LEATHER AND LACE

REBEL CARTER

VIOLET GAZE PRESS

Cover Design by Najla Qamber

Edited by Bria James & Jack Holloway

Published by Violet Gaze Press

20-22 Wenlock Rd

London

www.violetgazepress.com

❊ Created with Vellum

*For everyone who has ever had to fight
for their right to go their own way.*

CHAPTER 1

Mary Sophia James ran her brush through her hair for what felt like the thousandth time that morning, though the young lady could not be certain as she had lost count somewhere near the 740th stroke. How she had even managed to count her strokes for that long was a feat indeed but Mary had always found that counting did a world of good when it came to steadying her nerves.

Although in this instance, Mary's nerves were not the concern. Her unsettled stomach was.

She winced as the dry toast she had eaten that morning roiled and churned in her belly. She hadn't been able to keep much down for the past week. Mary had been determined to keep her black tea and toast precisely where it was meant to be. Her small figure was already feeling the loss of a week's breakfasts.

She winced and stopped, letting her brush hit the vanity in front of her with a clatter. Mary blanched at the bout of nausea that swept over her in ever-growing waves. It appeared her efforts in brushing her hair had amounted to nothing more than a head full of tended-to locks.

"Lord," she murmured, shoving away from the vanity and rushing towards the water basin a few feet away. There was no hope of her making it anywhere but the basin, not if she wanted to avoid making a mess of her day dress. Her mother, no doubt, would throw a fit worthy of publication if Mary ruined one of her few dresses, especially when they hadn't the funds to have it laundered at present.

The contents of Mary's stomach emptied into the basin with little incident and for that she was grateful. She slumped to the side, dabbing as delicately as she was able to at her mouth with the linen tea towel beside her. She sighed and pressed her fingers to her temples while she focused on breathing in-and-out in measured breaths.

"Calm, yourself. Be calm," she sighed with a shake of her head. "It will all be well. It will, it will, *it will...*"

Though for all of her self-soothing, Mary didn't believe a single word she was saying, and that was because things had little chance of working out for a woman such as she. Not in the world as it presently was, not with society's expectations and cruel enforcement of justice where women like her were concerned.

Women that had indulged in the pleasures of the flesh outside of wedlock. Women that had been, truthfully, too naive to truly understand the gravitas of what they were doing, women who had thought it was the *only way* to improve their station.

"Silly, *stupid* girl," Mary whispered, her voice almost as

bitter as the acrid taste of bile left on her tongue from that morning's sickness. She should have never done it, never given herself so freely to a man who had no intention of marrying her.

But what was she to do with her mother bearing down on her as she was, as she had always done since Mary was old enough to catch a man's eye? She was a lovely girl and had always managed to find favor from men of all manner and economic status. More than once Mary had thought herself capable of returning their affection and attention but some detail or another would come to light and her mother would deem the suitor perfectly unmarriable, and once more it was upon Mary's shoulders to find another suitor in possession of more wealth, more pedigree, more business savvy.

More...more...more...

It was always the case of more where her mother was concerned. Sarah James had never been one to settle.

"You shall never receive what you are due if you do not demand it," she informed her daughter daily. "Take what you want, Mary. You were born to it."

Except that Mary found she quite hated more. Her dresses always required more lace, her hair more ribbons, she was found lacking in graces and charms, her musical skills at the pianoforte and song always too stiff, her ability to carry a conversation flawlessly with sparkling laughter nonexistent, or at least if Sarah James was to be believed.

Her mother had married young and well above her station as the daughter of poor Irish immigrants. Her hands did not know manual labor as her mother's had, her fashionable clothing was the work of skilled modistes and designed to impress, unlike the plain muslin Sarah James had been raised in, and Mary's childhood home was nothing short of a palace when compared to the rickety walk-up in which her grandmother had raised nine children.

And then misfortune had struck by way of her father's untimely death at sea. This was what happened when a merchant fancied himself a sailor. Mary had begged her Papa not to captain the ship bound for South America, but he had not listened. It had been years since he had worked on a ship, but in his words it was, "As natural as breathing air. I shall be fine, Minnie. I'll be home in time for Christmas. You'll see, my Minnie."

Minnie.

Her heart wrenched painfully. It had been so long since anyone had called her that tender name. Her father had been a soft touch when it came to her, and she had relished it. Christmas had been their most treasured time together. Her father had always loved Christmas, and so had she until he had been taken away by the sea.

Mary closed her eyes, willing the tears not to fall. When the waves had swallowed his ship, they had also taken her future. Gone were her carefree days, ones that had once stretched on endlessly in front of her full of nothing but possibility. In their place was a ticking clock counting down the days and hours until what little remained of her father's estate dwindled to nothing. Successful merchant though he was, her father had been lax in making provision for the bulk of his assets---by fluke of law the lot had been taken by distant family Mary scarcely recognized. She supposed her father had always assumed she would marry affluently, had put off the endeavor hoping for a grandson, or son-in-law to deed his wealth to. But she had not married, thought she'd been in possession of plenty of time to take her pick of suitors. But she had been wrong.

So utterly wrong.

The family that had come to take their share of her father's wealth had reminded her of vultures. Greedy, beady-eyed things bent on taking and taking *and taking.* There had been no love lost between them and her mother, which had made it remarkably easy for said family to upend the grieving women's lives and leave Mary and her mother all but destitute save for what they were able to carry with them from their home.

There had been no kindness in those people, and they had killed whatever kindness, precious little as it was, that had once lived in her mother.

Mary slumped back against the table she sat in front of. After her morning sickness, she knew there was little chance that she did not look unwell. She did not wish to add red-eyed to the list of faults her mother would account to her during their daily walk about town. She sucked in a deep breath and rose shakily to her feet. She needed to freshen up and set herself to sorts. Nothing short of perfection would do for Sarah James.

She would meet her mother and do her best. She would perhaps dazzle her with a witty anecdote and though the Baptiste heir had slipped through her fingers there would be another well-suited man. One that had good intentions, one that she could, with effort, force herself to care for, to want as she…well, as she wanted women. Her fingers clutched at her skirts and she raised her hands to her belly. It was still trim, her skirts and corsets hiding what she and her mother knew, the proof of her one foray into trapping a man when she hadn't a cent to her name.

She had been willing, but she had thought it would garner her the name and place in a house as good as the one she'd been turned out of. That hadn't happened. The man and his offer had vanished, drying up like a spilled drink in the unyielding heat of the Texas sun. Why had she done as her mother instructed? The woman did not care for her, not like her father. No, never like that.

I'll be home in time for Christmas. You'll see, my Minnie.

It had been nearly a year since anyone had called her that term of affection. Almost four months since she had realized the clock above her head was now spinning wildly out of control. And she had no idea what her life would become once the secret of her delicate situation was made known to the public.

A bitter laugh escaped her mouth. It was not a situation. It was a pregnancy. One that she'd been ill-educated to anticipate, and now here she was fighting for her future with each and every simper and smile. She did not want a man, but she did, in fact, want her child. A hand dropped protectively over the spot she supposed it to be.

For it was not just one strike against Mary, but two. Yes, she was pregnant, and yes, she much preferred the gentle touch of women to the company of a man. Marriage or not, she would have damned the entire thing if she were able to, but there was no escaping her mother, not when her place at Sarah James's side was all she knew.

She hated it.

Mary turned to look at herself in the mirror and her resolve for perfection wavered. Her bottom lip quivered, and Mary lost her play at perfection. She burst into tears, arms wrapped around herself as she shook with sobs in the small room that was not hers, in the town she did not belong and in a life that she did not want.

CHAPTER 2

"Whatever is the matter with you? Please, do keep up, we haven't the time for your dilly-dallying, Mary." Sarah James's stern voice cut through Mary's pounding headache.

The pair were out on their daily walk about town, and Mary had been struggling to see through the blinding pain at her temples. It was difficult to keep up with her mother's brisk walk in the best of times, let alone when she was having difficulty walking in a straight line.

"I'm sorry, Mama. It's just that my head--"

"Stop dawdling, Mary Sophia." Her mother's tight grip tugged at her elbow and pulled her forward to match her step. "I heard there was a new batch of bankers and investors coming to town on account of Julian Baptiste's efforts with the railroad depot. If we make it to the cafe then we have a good chance at catching their eye."

Mary frowned, still rubbing at her temples. "What do you mean 'we'?"

Sarah James let out a titter of laughter and turned to

give Mary what she supposed was her mother's attempt at coquettish. "Well, two arrows are better than one, now aren't they dear?"

"Are you saying that you are intending on finding yourself a suitor?" Mary drew up to her full height despite the pain she suffered. "Are you aiming to marry again?"

"Keep your voice down! Good god, you would think I had never spent the money to send you to finishing school, screeching like a fish wife!" Her mother berated her at a volume far more at home in a saloon at midnight than on the town's main avenue at midday.

Mary glanced about furtively and stifled her groan at seeing the attention they were attracting. Her mother's near shouting was doing wonders at making them stand out in Gold Sky. She didn't estimate it was quite in the way her mother wished for them to gain attention.

"Now come along and do walk with your back straight. Remember your lessons on posture and grace for heaven's sake, Mary Sophia."

"Yes, Mama," Mary replied automatically. So oft had she said the words that her response fell from her lips with little thought. And for her part, Sarah James, so used to having her wishes fulfilled by her daughter, did not think twice at the barely there response.

"Now then, pinch your cheeks and I wish you had thought to apply a bit of rouge. You look so pale in the daylight. We simply must get you in the sun at more regular times."

At that Mary found her tongue. "I love the sun, but you say it causes freckles."

Sarah James clucked her teeth and nodded in agreement. "Right you are, right you are. The sun is no place for a woman like you."

Mary would have scoffed if her headache hadn't redoubled its efforts to lay her low. There would be no scoffing, not when she was nearly blinded by her pain and the sun overhead. Instead, Mary hurried along behind her mother, and before long the cafe her mother spoke of came into sight. She breathed a sigh of relief when her mother slowed her pace and let go of her arm.

"There it is. Lily's Cafe, or some such. It apparently has decent food, unlike the establishment we were turned out of, like common riffraff," her mother gave an indignant sniff. Mary bit back the remark about their behavior, her mother's in particular towards Julian Baptiste's new bride. The cook had been nothing but efficient, her meals tasty, and she'd always had a smile for her when her mother's back was turned.

Mary's cheeks burned with shame thinking on how she had kept her mouth shut when she should have spoken out. Of how she had followed her mother's lead in attitude and decorum towards the other woman. It was hard to remember who she was when her mother's hand was so tight on her neck. It was as if the older woman's grip tightened as surely as Mary's corset and stays did with each and every day of growth.

A hand strayed to her belly and she sighed when it growled. She was hungry, no doubt due to her morning sickness. If she were lucky her mother would allow her the time to eat...maybe if she did manage to catch a man's eye, then she would be invited to lunch with him? The thought perked her up and she lifted her head to see that her mother's keen eyes were, for once, not on her.

Now her mother's emerald gaze was trained on a far bigger prize than Mary.

"Bankers," her mother breathed, hands practically rubbing together in anticipation, "and lots of them. Come close, and quick Mary. We will have to pick out the one for you."

"I don't feel well, mother," Mary said but her daughter's protestations fell on deaf ears, Sarah James waving a hand at her.

"Pish. Stand up straight and smile, dear. Men like a woman who smiles."

Mary clenched her jaw tight. She didn't trust herself to keep her mouth shut without the extra effort and fortunately, her mother mistook it for smiling.

"Now, then, that one looks quite good. He's young. That means he won't understand what's *happening* until it's too late."

The happening was the baby. The baby that Mary wanted. She had begun to tire of hearing of her child in the abstract, or as a thing---or even worse, a problem.

"It's a child, mother. Not a 'happening,'" Mary blurted out before she thought better of it. She clapped a hand over her mouth with a muffled gasp once she realized what she'd done. The words fell fat and heavy in the dirt between them with a nearly audible thud. Mary blinked and watched as her mother slowly turned to her, the older woman's face was nearly red with frustration.

"Watch your tongue, girl."

"Yes, mother."

Sarah James sucked in a deep calming breath and ran a hand over her skirts with a shake of her head. "On better thought, I think it may be best that I go, on my own."

"Your own?" Mary asked in confusion. Her mother allowed for so little alone time that the suggestion surprised her.

"Yes, alone. I see an older gentleman in the bunch that I think would quite enjoy an introduction. You may use this time to do as you please."

"Truly?" Mary's heart soared with joy and for a moment she forgot about her painful headache. Who knew when her mother would next leave her with a moment's peace? The moment must be seized and savored, enjoyed to the fullest in whatever small way she could find in this frontier town.

"Yes, truly. It's not as if anything worse can happen to you," her mother bit out, giving her daughter a cold look. The words should have stung, but Mary found they didn't so much. Not when there was the promise of an after-noon hour spent away from Sarah James.

Her mother stepped closer to her and lowered her voice so that none but they could hear her words. "Now stay out of trouble for the next hour, hmm? I will return with lunch for you, courtesy of the rich gentleman I have in my sights, if all goes well."

She balked at her mother's assertion that the man in question had money, how could one even tell such a thing from a glance? She had known more men than she could count that dressed as a dandy, though they proved penni-less and feckless in business matters. Her father had warned her against tolerating the attentions of such men, *and yet here she was all the same.*

She wrapped her arms around herself, shoving away the dark thought. She forced a smile as fake as any she sent her mother's way and nodded quickly.

"Yes, mother."

Sarah James came to touch her daughter's cheek lightly, a hand cupping it briefly though the woman's eyes were still not on Mary. She did not see her daughter, not now and not ever. She tapped Mary's cheek lightly before she was gliding away again, her voice rising as she walked away.

"Have a good time, darling."

Mary raised her hand in farewell, a genuine smile, the first to grace her lips in quite some time. "Enjoy your meal, Mama!"

Sarah James raised an eyebrow at her daughter's sudden cheeriness, but the woman said nothing and in a moment she had swept into the crowd of bankers. Mary watched in fascination as her mother introduced herself to the man she had chosen, one hand extended to him while the other was pressed demurely to her chest. The man rushed forward to instantly take her mother's hand and that was all Mary allowed herself to watch before she turned on her heel and set off down the avenue. She was certain her mother's plan for the man would proceed as she willed it. There was no sense in wasting her precious free time to witness it.

Mary walked forward with a smile on her lips. She was free. Well and truly, if even only for an hour.

"What to do, what to do?" she mused, swinging her

hands happily. She turned to look down the avenue and saw the public square bursting with activity. Townsfolk were hurrying to and fro with full arms and hands. An assortment of tables and benches stood in the normally neat and tidy square. A stage was being built at the center of it, the red maple tree planted there, though small, served as the perfect backdrop.

She took a step forward, eyes on the workers quickly putting together the stage, her mind on what sort of music she might hear that night if she was able to talk her mother into an outing. If her time with the new banker went well, Mary wagered she had as good a chance as any to convince Sarah James that a town event would be just the thing to celebrate her new introduction to 'a gentleman of means.' Surely the pair would need a place to celebrate their acquaintance, plus there was the added benefit that her mother could--

"Excuse me, miss." A voice interrupted Mary's scheming and she turned with a start.

"Oh, I'm sorry, I didn't see you there."

Because you were laying plans to get your way, like your mother.

Her cheeks burned bright at the voice that was growing louder by the day. What if it was right? What if she was every bit her mother's daughter and prone to schemes and well-crafted plans? What if the girl she had been under her father's care had been nothing more than a figment of circumstance, and not who she truly was?

"No trouble. I have a habit of appearing unexpectedly." The speaker, a woman, a whole head taller than she and solidly built. The woman had a neat bob, her chin length sleek blonde hair framing her face prettily. She had wide brown eyes, full lips and a dusting of freckles that lent an air of sweetness to a woman that otherwise seemed anything but. There was a look to her that spoke of strength. The simple outfit of work trousers and a white work shirt made of thick durable material rolled up her forearms, thick leather work gloves covered her hands and a red bandana hung from the woman's neck perfectly setting off her blonde hair. If Mary was to wax poetic she might even liken the woman to the Montana frontier.

Raw. Beautiful. Wild.

"I just, ah, need to get past you to the stage there, miss." The woman held up the bundle of lumber in her arms and Mary jumped to attention. Here she had been gawking like a love-struck girl, while the woman had been trying to go about her business and with a load of lumber no less!

"I apologize. I was dawdling. Awful habit of mine," Mary explained, hurrying to get out of the woman's way and she winced when the beautiful blonde fixed her with a curious look. "And now I'm blathering on as well. I--can I help?" Mary offered when she could think of nothing else to say. She should be silent and leave her to her work but wished with her entire being to stay close to the woman.

She watched with bated breath as the woman walked past, head high and arms strong. She turned her head to look at Mary, a wide smile on her full lips. They were blush pink like the roses in the family garden in Texas. How she used to love those fresh cut flowers before the summer wilted them.

15

"You are a lady. I could not ask you to dirty your hands, miss."

"I am no lady," Mary laughed, and against her better judgment, fell in to step behind the woman. She could be bothering her; Sarah James would be quick to point out that Mary certainly was, but until she was told so she could pretend that the woman enjoyed her company.

"I have a nose for ladies, and you are a lady. Frontier is an odd place to find one as fine as you."

"You're a lady, too."

The blonde grinned and set down the load of lumber she was carrying beside the frame of the stage. She pulled off her gloves and gave them a shake, slapping them against her thigh.

"What is your name?" she asked, eyes lowered purposefully on her gloves.

"Mary. Mary Sophia James."

"That's a beautiful name." The woman raised her eyes to Mary's. "The kind made for beautiful ladies."

Mary blushed. Her heartbeat quickened in her chest at the words, and if she was not mistaken there was a gleam of something familiar in the woman's warm brown eyes that beckoned her forward. She knew that look, the furtive, quiet, but telling look of a woman *noticing her.*

How she had dreamed of finding that look in the one she wed.

The woman tucked her gloves into the pocket of the trousers she wore. "My name is Alex. Alex Pierce."

Mary's brow furrowed. "Alex?"

"Short for Alexandria. My mother had an unhealthy

love for all things Egyptian, you know, as all upper-crust women of her age and predilection were want to do."

Mary laughed and nodded, remembering her own mother's craze over the beautiful Egyptian items many of their peers had shown off in their homes. Her father had forbidden it, firmly deciding the lot of it was theft, much to her mother's dismay.

Mary had always thought her father right, but now that she was looking upon Alex, she was glad that the craze had led to one thing of beauty. Alexandria suited the woman in front of her so perfectly she could think of no other name so beautiful. She looked away quickly and smiled, willing the adoration she felt welling up in her to abate.

"Your name is lovely. I am happy to make your acquaintance."

Alex gave her another smile and inclined her head. "And I am happy to make yours Mary."

"Call me, Minnie." The request fell from her lips faster than she could process it and she blinked in shock at herself, though Alex paid no mind to it and nodded.

"Minnie, then. Are you new to town? I've not seen you around I'm afraid."

"Yes, I am. I only arrived a few weeks back."

"Are you alone?"

Mary shook her head. "No, I am here with my mother. We are looking at settling in the area."

"Curious place to think of settling. Two ladies on their own in a place like Gold Sky."

"How do you mean?" Mary asked as she tucked her hands behind her. There was a knowing tone in Alex's voice that caught her attention and she leaned forward waiting for the woman to continue speaking.

"People come to Gold Sky to escape their past. To get away from whatever bad is holding them down in the normal world."

Mary's mouth dropped open at Alex's no-nonsense words and clear reading of her situation. But how did the woman know she was running, or rather being dragged by her mother, from her troubles?

"You sound as if you know from experience," Mary observed, and Alex raised a shoulder in a shrug.

"I do. I'm no different than any seeking refuge from their past. Gold Sky is my escape, same as most here."

"Same as me?" Mary asked. She held her breath waiting for Alex to respond. The blonde tucked her hair behind her ear and ambled forward with a curt nod.

"Of course, same as you. We are all in search of a safe place to land, and Gold Sky is that for me. Must be something mighty big for you and your mama to come alone. Perhaps someone?" Alex rocked back on her heels, that same knowing tone in her voice but this time it had Mary rushing to answer.

"Not my Papa. He's long gone, he passed," she said.

Alex's eyes widened slightly. "I'm sorry for your loss. A loss like that can force a move...is that what prompted your search for a new home?"

"In a way," Mary hedged. She clasped her hands and dropped her eyes much preferring the sight of her shoes to the earnest look in Alex's eyes. If she looked too long, she might say a good deal more than she should to a stranger. That would not be a good idea. No matter how beautiful they were.

"We need a new home and this place is as good as any," she finished when Alex continued to look at her with brown eyes she knew saw far too much.

Alex hummed. "Fair point. The town is quite hospitable to all people, no matter their lifestyle."

Lifestyle. Now that piqued her interest. "What do you mean by that?" Mary asked.

"I mean to say people are free to live as they choose here. Free to *love* and live as they choose. Free to be the person they wanted but were never allowed to be where they came from."

"Oh." Mary swallowed hard and looked up at her. "And what truth were you allowed to live in Gold Sky that the world denied you before?"

"My right to love who I choose," Alex replied. Mary blinked and looked towards the other woman. They were still standing beside the stage, but now Alex moved away from the structure, away from the other workers and Mary was powerless to stay where she was. Wordlessly she followed behind Alex, straining to hear the other woman when she began speaking again.

"Do you really want to know?" Alex asked, her voice was gentle and soft. Words measured.

"Yes, of course," Mary breathed as they came to a stop a fair distance away from the hustle and bustle of the town square. They were alone now, at the far end beside the church where it was quieter. It was a pretty little church, painted white with windows framing the double doors, a steepled tower held a bell that Mary knew rang sweet and true. Alex ambled towards the steps and dusted off the bottom with a sweep of her work gloves.

"Would you care to sit?" she asked, gesturing towards the step.

Mary smiled at her. "Thank you," she murmured, taking her seat. She had not been treated so kindly since society had estimated her in possession of a large fortune. It did more than its fair share to kindle a warmth in her, one that was entirely aimed at Alex, and Alex alone. When she sat, the other woman came forward and sat beside her on the step. They were still far enough apart that they were respectable to any that looked upon them, though Mary had found women often were able to skirt the lines of respectability because theirs was a love not many recognized. An attraction such as that was allowed to exist under the guise of friendship and a closeness particular to women. But any who knew where to look knew different.

Mary was one such person. She prayed Alex was as well.

When they were settled and quiet for a moment, Alex began speaking. "I came to Gold Sky out of necessity," she said. 'I was not born to a family as accepting as I would have hoped. Though by the same measure I expect I am not the daughter my family hoped for."

Mary frowned and turned to look at Alex. The blonde was staring straight ahead, her eyes on the workers still setting up in the town square. There was no image finer than the sight of Alexandria Pierce's profile warmed by the glow of the early afternoon sunlight, even with her beautiful features as somber as they were.

"I am interested only in the fairer sex, and that is a wrong my family could not forgive."

Mary's back straightened with a snap. "A wrong? What do you mean to say? It is not something you can control or choose, it just is."

A smile spread over Alex's face and she turned her head to look at Mary. "Oh, I know that. Glad to know you think so too. It is not us that are ignorant, but our families."

Mary crossed her arms with a shake of her head. "It isn't fair. None of it is fair, and they expect us to simply pretend that nothing is--" her words stopped and she blinked, realizing what she had been saying, what secret she had just exposed to a near stranger. "I mean to say that in theory," she said weakly.

Alex hummed. "In theory, yes, but something tells me it isn't all theory for you. Is that why you've come to Gold Sky?" Warm brown eyes met Mary's green at the question, and she twisted her hands in her skirts.

"No, not, I mean not…" her voice trailed off and she winced, sucking in a deep breath at her jumbled explanation. "I mean that it isn't *just that*," she finally finished.

Alex leaned back elbows braced on the step behind her. "So it is that, at least partly then?"

"Well, ah, yes. It is, but Mama isn't so concerned about that. She was convinced I would marry well in spite of my desires. She's far more concerned about another matter altogether."

Alex pursed her full lips. "And what might that be?"

Mary shook her head and twisted her hands together. "I can't say."

"Whatever it is, I assure you it is not as shameful as you think. You are not a bad person, no matter what people have led you to believe."

Mary laughed bitterly and looked away. "You scarcely know me, and I, you. Just because I am taken with you does not--"

"You're taken with me?" Alex abandoned her relaxed pose and sat up to face Mary. "I suspected as much."

"Yes, if you must know, and I am not ashamed of it."

"That's right fortunate as I find myself equally taken with you, Minnie."

Her heart squeezed at the casual drop of her name. *Minnie.* She found she loved the sound of the name on Alex's lips.

"I like the way my name sounds coming from your mouth," she confessed. The admission made Alex's cheeks flush and the woman chuckled, the low and slow sound of it making Mary's toes curl in her boots.

"Never had a lady tell me something pretty like that."

"I told you before. I'm no lady."

Alex rested her hand in the space between them. She moved it then, to the side, hand sliding until it was nearly brushing the edge of Mary's skirts. "Liar," she said, but her voice was light and teasing, the sound of it making Mary smile.

"For some reason I do not guard my words with you," Mary said. "Scarcely an hour and I've already told you a secret."

"And I you. Concerning, isn't it?"

"Truly, but you already knew that, didn't you?" Mary asked. She was never this...direct, hadn't been in quite some time and she liked the feel of it. Like an older worn and loved coat, a favorite that she had lost track of and that she had now found. She reveled in the familiar feel of it.

"I did, I did," Alex admitted with a grin and a wink. "I would be lying if I didn't admit I hoped for such a secret when I first saw you, but the second secret is a different matter altogether."

"Ah, yes...that." Mary smiled ruefully. "I should guard my words, but it has been a long time since I have been able to speak so freely. I feel more myself and that is because of you. Thank you, Alex." She looked down to where Alex's hand still rested beside hers and hesitated before moving it closer.

"My pleasure, Minnie." Her hand inched ever closer until their pinkies touched and Mary sucked in her breath. "You can keep talking to me. I'll not breathe a word of it to another soul."

"Why would you do that for me?"

"Because once upon a time, someone did that for me, and it made me who I am." Their pinkies slid against the other in a gentle stroke. Mary's hand tensed at the gentle brush of Alex's finger, but she relaxed a moment later and scooted closer to her.

"I'm pregnant," she whispered, voice thick with emotion. "My mother brought us here after I proved inept at securing a marriage to the father." She frowned and sighed quietly. "I never did understand men very well, but that is...to be expected."

"Men are challenging. Women are not."

Mary smiled at the gentle stroking of Alex's finger

against hers. It was soothing in the very best way and it kept her talking when she knew she should have kept her mouth shut.

"I don't know about that. I've known quite a few challenging women in my time, but they do come with less...complications," she said, her free hand coming to rest on her stomach.

"You don't have to keep running. It doesn't matter if you have the baby." Alex paused and swallowed. "Do you wish to keep the baby?"

"Yes, with all my heart," Mary answered in earnest. "The father meant nothing to me, not in any sense of the word. I did what I did because of my mother."

"Your mother?"

Mary gave a quick nod, just a tilt of her chin but it was a nod all the same. "Yes, my mother. She has certain expectations for me and for us. She thinks Gold Sky will be a new place for us to start over but in order for that to happen--"

"You need a husband."

"Yes." Mary bit her lip. "It's a complicated thing."

"I don't know about that," Alex replied, and she moved until she was covering Mary's hand with hers. Alex's hand was warm, gentle, and most of all strong. She could practically feel the strength radiating from Alex and into her from that simple point of contact. Mary sighed in relief welcoming the grounding touch. She turned her hand up so that they were touching palm to palm.

"Why do you say that?" she asked.

"If you need to be married that's one thing, but why must it be to a man?"

Mary's eyebrows rose in surprise at the question. "Because I am only allowed to marry a man?" she asked in some confusion, but from the snort Alex gave her she wondered if there was another solution she had not considered.

"Not in Gold Sky. You know of its accepting nature, yes?"

Mary blinked in surprise. She had heard stories of the town's progressive stance, knew firsthand from seeing the way people lived here. Why there was even a woman with two husbands! But what did that mean when it came to her and her situation?

"What do you mean?" she asked when she trusted her voice not to waver.

"In Gold Sky there is more than one way to be married, Minnie, and one of those ways is *without* a man."

CHAPTER 3

"*W*hat are you--"

"Mary!" Her mother's shrill shout cut through the din of activity around them and sliced into the little piece of solitude and peace Mary had found with Alex. She looked with a start to see her mother marching across the square.

The woman paid no mind to the workers around her, and more than one shout of caution and disapproving look followed in Sarah James's wake. She was carrying a covered basket in her hands and Mary remembered she was practically starved. How could her hour already be up? And when there was so much to talk over with Alex as well. It was just her luck her mother arriving at this moment.

She had to find a way to continue the conversation and fast. It had all felt so big, momentous in what Alex was about to disclose and she could not let it slip through her fingers now. And speaking of fingers and hands...Mary jerked her hand back from where it still lay beneath Alex's. She curled her hand into a fist and pressed it to her chest with an apologetic look at the woman beside her.

"That's my mother," she told Alex. "I did not expect her to arrive so suddenly. She will not let us continue speaking. Not if she sees us like this." She shook her head and continued, breath catching as she rushed to get the words out. "I wager she would refuse us the opportunity to speak even if she did not understand what I feel towards you. But I must know what you were about to tell me."

"About the peculiarities of marriage and Gold Sky?"

"Yes, that. Please." Mary gave a quick jerk of her chin.

"There is a dance tonight. We can meet there and speak. I will be there as an usher. Do you think you can manage to convince her?"

Mary bit her lip and glanced towards her mother who was waving at her now and yelling her name with new vigor. The covered platter in her hands was a good sign that her lunch had gone well. Mary could work with that.

"I will do it."

"Then meet me here," Alex tapped the step they sat on with a rap of her knuckle, "at the church tonight at seven. I'll be waiting even if she keeps you. I'll explain it all then." Alex stood and gave her a meaningful look. "You are not a bad person, Minnie. You are just a desperate one. Remember that."

And then Alex was turning on her heel and walking away. She crossed paths with her mother, but the older woman barely spared her a glance in her trek forward.

"What are you doing sitting here? You were supposed

to meet me at the cafe. I've been looking all over for you, young lady."

"My feet were tired, mama. Back too. I had to sit for a moment so that I didn't faint," Mary explained, standing from her seat. She was loath to leave the spot and her mother made a shushing motion with a hand.

"Stop carrying on or people will think something's wrong with you." She thrust the covered dish at her daughter. "Here is your lunch provided by my own hard work."

"Lunch was successful then?" she asked, flipping back the covering of the platter to reveal a side of roast beef, potatoes, two yeast rolls and a slice of chocolate cake. Her mouth watered looking down at it all and it took all of her willpower not to snatch a roll up and shove it in her mouth at once.

"Very, as you can see by these generous provisions. I let him know my daughter was feeling under the weather. Mr. Rutherford sends his regards, darling. Now come along." She flicked a finger at Mary, beckoning her to follow behind and set off towards the boarding house they were staying in.

Mary fell in step behind her mother but not before sneaking a quick bite of the roll. She almost moaned in satisfaction. It was absolute perfection.

"The sir is unattached and well-spoken, in possession of considerable fortune and gumption. I estimate his worth to be twice what your father's was."

Mary's head snapped up at that. "I wish you wouldn't speak of Papa like that."

"Like what?" Her mother turned to glare at her, and

Mary swallowed hard, the once tasty morsel of food turning to ash in her mouth at having her mother's piercing eyes focused on her.

"Like he was nothing more than a means to an end. Like he was an investment bond," Mary's voice shook, but she continued speaking. She had loved her father and he loved her. She knew he had treated her mother well despite their differences, and she could not abide Sarah James's mercenary tone when speaking of him now that he was gone.

"He was a good man."

Sarah James's eyebrows drew together, and she turned away. "Yes, he was," she said, her voice soft and gentle in a way that Mary hadn't heard in years. Perhaps her mother missed her father as much as Mary did? She frowned and opened her mouth, ready to offer comfort to her but then Sarah James did what she did best and reminded her that she was not a soft woman.

"And he was too gentle with you. He spent all that money on giving you a fine education and look at where you ended up. He spoiled you." Mary jerked back as if she had been slapped and nearly dropped the platter of food in her hands as her mother continued. "But none of that matters now. Mr. Rutherford seems to be of the same mind as I. He will need a respectable wife, especially in his dealings with the community at large and I aim to be the most attractive candidate."

"Of course, mama."

"Now then, inside with you. I have a plan to hatch." She gestured at the boarding house in front of which they stood. It was a modest two-story establishment, not as fine as Ms. Alice Hill's but still far better than Mary had thought the frontier could offer by way of lodging. She was simply happy they had no need to stay in the town saloon.

"What kind of plan?" Mary asked. She was grateful for an opportunity to sit and eat but hated to leave the warm sunshine and company of other people behind. She glanced behind her one last time taking in the sight of the life Gold Sky had to offer. Around her there were all manner of people, fair and dark skinned alike, and all of them seemed to be...*happy.*

How she wished for a bit of that for herself. But did she deserve it still?

You are not a bad person, Minnie. You are just a desperate one.

She sighed heavily. Alex's words worked as a balm to her nerves and she turned to follow her mother into the boarding house. She shut the door and continued forward to see her mother's skirts vanishing into the dining room. Wordlessly she followed and took her place at the dining table. Her mother dropped a set of silverware beside her before taking a seat across the table, but even with a fork and knife at hand Mary knew better than to eat. Not until her mother gave her word that she was free to do so.

"What is your plan, mother?" she asked.

"To make Mr. Rutherford fall in love with me of course. I want the man besotted and proposing within the week. If I plan carefully, I think I can manage it."

"The week? Why so soon?"

"On account of your little situation." Her mother gave her abdomen a pointed look. "We have no clue how long until you begin to show that you are expecting, now do we? The sooner that I am able to secure an offer of marriage the better. It will also make getting a man interested in you all the easier if there is an influential man attached to us."

Mary nodded, eyes on her plate. "Of course, mama." Her mind already turning over the puzzle of how she would persuade her mother to attend the town festivities.

"...But of course, the gentleman has already asked for me to accompany him to the fair this evening and--Mary are you listening to me at all?"

"Pardon?" Mary blinked in surprise.

"Do stop daydreaming and pay attention to me, and for heaven's sake eat your food." She waved a hand at Mary, and despite the disapproving look on her face, Mary had never heard a sweeter word from her mother.

"Yes, mama." She snatched up her silverware and set to work eating her lunch with fervor. It was good to eat and have something in her belly to chase away the memory of sickness. It was only when she was halfway through her roast beef that she remembered she was supposed to be listening to her mother's thoughts on the 'gentleman of means'.

"He expects me to attend the fair like a common woman."

"Aren't you?" Mary asked in confusion but at the dark look on her mother's face she quickly added. "I mean to say that it would be good for Mr. Rutherford to see you as a salt of the earth woman. No doubt he has had his fair share of, ah, women in search of wealth. If you give him the impression that he has found a woman unconcerned with appearances and the like, then he may find you more desirable."

Mary hated that she knew the exact words to say to manipulate her mother into attending the fair, but it was necessary. She did not wish for it, but she was desperate. It was a means to an end and hopefully she would not have to do it again once she knew what Alex had to tell her.

"Too true, too true." Sarah James nodded in agreement. "Then you are of the opinion that I should attend the fair this evening?"

"Yes, of course. If your aim is to secure a proposal then as much time spent in his company is best, but do not, ah, do not go alone," she continued on, remembering that she must get herself to the fair as well.

"What do you mean?" Sarah James gave her a shrewd look that Mary knew well from having it trained on her more times than she could count.

"I mean that I should come with you, to the fair. If you were to go alone then it would present an odd picture to the gentleman."

"He thinks you are sick. There is no reason for you to attend, and we do not have the spare money to provide you with any refreshments," Sarah James countered.

A shiver of panic rose up in Mary at her mother's words. She had to go to the fair. She simply must and if she meant to sneak out there, she knew her luck would not hold. There was no way her mother would not spot her Titian hair in the crowd that night.

"I do not need refreshments. This meal is plenty to

tide me over until breakfast. I swear it." Mary gestured to the plate in front of her.

"Why do you wish to go to the fair so badly tonight? I think there is something you are not telling me, dear." Her mother leaned back in her chair and crossed her arms. "What is it you want so badly?"

"Nothing!" Mary blurted out and winced at the desperate tone in her voice. "I mean, nothing, mama. Nothing. I only wish for you to have the best opportunity with the gentleman. I can help provide that. It is my, ah, future on the line as well. We both know you are far better suited to securing a match than I." She set her fork down and smiled as sincerely as she could. "I only wish to help, mama. I swear it."

Sarah James steepled her fingers and considered her. "I suppose a family image would go a long way when enticing a man to see me in a kinder, gentler manner."

"It would. You would show Mr. Rutherford that you are able to offer him more than simply a pretty smile, but a partner capable of making a home for him. That is the true dream for any man of business."

Sarah James dropped her hands and smiled at her daughter. It was nothing more than a show of teeth, but it was far more than Mary was accustomed to seeing.

"And all this time I thought you woefully inept at understanding the finer points of society and relationships. I underestimated you, Mary. I am impressed by your keen thinking."

"Thank you, mama. I learned from you."

"Good to know that you are paying some attention." Her mother practically beamed at her and then tapped the table as if settling the matter entirely. "Now then, you will come with me to the fair. We leave at seven sharp. A lady never keeps a man waiting and we shall be escorted to the event by Mr. Rutherford and his associates. Is that understood?"

Mary nodded forcing a cheery smile to her face. "Yes, I will be ready and eager to make his acquaintance."

Sarah James nodded and rose from the table. "Finish your meal and do wear the green dress. It suits your complexion and eyes perfectly. That is all." Her mother took her leave and Mary sighed in relief the second she rounded the corner and turned down the hallway.

She had secured her way to the fair, but she would not be on time to meet Alex, though at least she knew the woman would wait. She had told her as much, hadn't she?

"Calm yourself," she whispered, pressing her hand to her chest. "She will wait, she will wait. She said so." Mary sucked in a deep breath and rubbed her chest until she was able to take in a solid breath. She lifted her head up and nodded once her heartbeat had slowed enough for her to concentrate.

"She will wait." Mary picked up her fork and knife and began to cut into her meal again. "She will wait. She will."

CHAPTER 4

"You cleaned up nicely. Well done, Mary." Sarah James gave her an approving nod as she looked her daughter over. "Mr. Rutherford will be impressed by how well the James family presents themselves."

"Thank you, mama." Mary hated that she felt the glow of pleasure in her chest. She should not warm to her mother's praise, but it was difficult for a girl not to want her mother's approval, no matter how dire or ill the circumstances.

A rap at the door signaled an arrival. Sarah James waved her daughter forward with a flick of her wrist. "Answer the door, dear and remember to smile.'

Mary gave her mother an absent-minded nod and went for the door. She opened it with little ceremony and could practically hear her mother's sigh of exasperation at her daughter's lack of fanfare and drama. Even so, she plastered a smile on her face and greeted the man in front of her with an incline of her head.

The man was tall and thin, his lean form clothed in fine bespoke clothing she knew had attracted her mother's attention. He wore his salt and pepper hair neatly combed, shoes polished until they gleamed and when he lifted his hand to his chest in greeting his silver cufflinks shone in the waning light. He smiled at her, and it was not an unkind smile she saw from the soft look in his blue eyes.

Perhaps the man would be a decent match for her mother. It would be a blessing to know he would not treat her unkindly. It would give Mary's nerves a much-needed break if she were able to rest assured in her mother's future.

"Hello, Miss. I am Reginald Rutherford. You are the younger Miss James, I presume?"

She bobbed her head in acknowledgement. "Yes, and I am pleased to make your acquaintance. I apologize for my illness keeping me from a lovely lunch this afternoon."

"Everyone must take time to rest. I am happy you have recovered." He bent low in a bow and surprised her when he took her hand and pressed a kiss to it. The man was grand in his gestures, her mother would adore it all.

"I have, I have." She turned her head to look behind her to where her mother stood and opened the door wider. "My mother and I are happy to spend the evening in your company. Aren't we mother?"

Sarah James swept forward with a smile on her face. "Yes, we are, dear." She extended a hand towards Mr. Rutherford. "Pleased to see you again, sir." The smile on her mother's face was unlike the few Mary was accustomed to seeing. This one was all tender and playful and made her mother appear infinitely younger than she was.

The transformation transfixed Mary to no end.

She forced herself to step aside while her mother and her suitor made their hellos and before long they were off and walking towards the town square. Her mother arm-in-arm with Mr. Rutherford while Mary trailed behind them. She pretended to be interested in the couple's pleasantries and was able to keep up a constant stream of chatter, but her eyes were sweeping the avenue as they walked.

She told herself it was on account of her taking in her new surroundings, but in truth she scanned the area looking for Alex. As much as she willed herself to believe the other woman would wait for her, she worried Alex would think she was not coming. If Mary saw her in passing she could attempt to catch her eye and be able to stop her from leaving entirely.

At least she hoped so.

"Darling, are you listening to a word I've said?"

Mary nearly winced and slowly looked back to her mother. "Pardon, mama?"

"I said, my darling girl, we will take a turn about the festivities and then perhaps meet back here within an hour's time?"

"Oh, only an hour? I was hoping for more?" Mary felt confident in her play for time. There was no way her mother would push back in front of her suitor. It would destroy the carefully crafted image of the good-natured mother she was working to create.

Sarah James raised her eyebrow at her daughter. "And what do you intend to do with such idleness, hmm?"

"I, ah, was hoping to enjoy the fair, of course, mama." She gestured towards the town square that had been cheerily decorated. Ribbons hung from shop balconies, there were lanterns dotting the space lending their warm light to the dusky sky. There were tables laden with food and drink nearby and at the center of the square a makeshift dance floor was in front of the stage where a band was playing merrily away.

If she wasn't mistaken, she even glimpsed what looked like a vaudeville strongman act taking place near the church. There was much to see and even without her plans to meet Alex. An hour's time would not be nearly enough to see and enjoy it all.

Sarah James narrowed her eyes at her daughter. "I don't see why you would--"

"Oh, I think some extra time would do the young lady good, don't you? There are so many new people to meet, and not to mention," he gave her mother a warm smile, "it would be lovely to spend more than an hour's time in your fair company, Sarah James."

Her mother paused and then blushed before she cleared her throat. "Yes, yes, you are quite right. More than an hour's time to enjoy the fair would do us all good, I think." She nodded at Mary. "Enjoy yourself, darling and do return here in, ah, two hours' time."

Mr. Rutherford beamed at her mother and then winked at Mary. "Enjoy yourself, young lady."

"Yes, sir." She smiled at him; this time it was genuine for his intervention allowed her the luxury of extra time.

Perhaps, having a man in her mother's sights would not be an altogether unpleasant thing.

"Have a merry time!" Mary waved at the couple. She kept her warm smile in place until they had turned and gone on their way. She stood still for a moment making sure they had well and truly disappeared into the crowd of merrymakers before she turned to rush towards the chapel. She was practically running as she broke through the crowd and she came to a stumbling stop at the foot of the steps.

And there, just as promised, stood Alex.

"What is it?" Alex asked, giving Mary a curious look. "You've been staring at me like you think I might up and fly away for the past ten minutes."

Mary flushed and dropped her eyes. "I didn't think you were going to be here. I mean because I was late to arrive and all."

Alex lifted her shoulder in a shrug. "I told you I would wait for you, and I am a woman of my word. Follow me, we can talk inside where your mama can't see."

"Oh, yes, clever thinking." Mary managed to return her smile though she was acutely aware that she hadn't been thinking of her mother or the danger that would come were Sarah James to see her with Alex. The woman was as breathtaking as she had been that afternoon, perhaps even more so with the dark of night around them, her features awash in the warm light of the lit lanterns, two on either side of her illuminating the stairs of the chapel. A ribbon garland snapped in the wind behind Alex, the pastels and lace of the decoration softening the woman's sharp profile.

Alex looked just as Mary had always imagined a knight in shining armor might appear. Reassuring looks, stoic profile, and her strong frame was enough to make a woman swoon like any respectable maiden fair. But if Alex were the knight and she the damsel fair, then what did that make her mother? Not a witch, but most assuredly the dragon. Mary's lips turned up in a smile and she came forward when Alex jerked a thumb over her shoulder towards the chapel doors.

"This way, Minnie." The couple entered the chapel easy as you please with not even the doors to the building being locked.

When Mary looked surprised Alex said, "No need to lock much up here. Not in this town. The people all know each other, though," she paused moving to the door as Mary walked in and passed her. "I expect that will change in the future with all the new arrivals, but for now the town remains as it is. How it changes can only remain to be seen."

Mary twisted her fingers in her skirts. "My mama and I are part of those new arrivals you think will change the town, aren't we?"

"Not you. Your mother, maybe but that's just the way of things." She shut the door and walked towards Mary with a wave of her hands. "Now then, we have important things to discuss don't we?"

Mary blinked at the sudden change of conversation, but Alex was right. There were far more important things to talk of instead of Mary's worry that she was once more a problem. If there was a way to make a life and home for herself in a new place, she wanted it, and if that place happened to be Gold Sky she wanted to make it the best place she could.

"Yes, that's right. What, ah, what were you going to tell me? I couldn't stop thinking about it. I've been trying to puzzle it out for hours now. Please tell me."

"Have a seat, Minnie." Alex swept a hand to a nearby pew and settled herself down. "I feel like this conversation might require you to be sitting."

"And why would that be? Is it because it is a salacious conversation?" Mary asked earnestly, taking a seat beside Alex.

Alex chuckled and crossed her arms. "Could be that you lose the ability to stand once the worries of your present situation are lifted from your shoulders. It's hard to remember how to stand when you aren't carrying such a heavy burden. Might think you'll float away."

"If only that were possible. I'd have floated away a long time ago."

"That I believe, but you might find you do once I tell you that I have figured out a solution to your situation."

Mary was practically bouncing in her seat with anticipation, but she forced herself to remain still and patient. She managed it, but only just.

"When I told you that marriage in Gold Sky did not require a man I meant that you would be free to find a woman that suited your taste. That you need not resign yourself to a lie for the rest of your life."

"What do you mean, I would be able to marry a

woman? Such a thing is not possible. It's difficult to even remain unattached and in the company of a woman that does strike one's fancy. How would I manage a marriage?"

"What do you know of Gold Sky?" Alex asked.

Mary considered the question for a moment and thought about what her Mother had told her about the town. There had been a considerable amount of information Sarah James had drilled into her head but most of it had surrounded Julian Baptiste's whereabouts and preferences. She frowned when she realized she did not know much else than what she had gleaned from her brief outings to the mercantile or church.

"Well, I know that the town is growing and rapidly so. The new railroad depot Julian Baptiste is bringing to Gold Sky has put it on the map as a destination for investors."

Alex nodded approvingly at her. "That is right. We are quite busy as of late and we have Mr. Baptiste to thank for it. He's a fair man interested in the town's well-being on account of his new wife and his sister's roots in the town. What else do you know?"

"Ah, well his sister is the teacher?" Mary tried when she could think of nothing else.

"Yes, that's right. Do you know anything about her marriage?"

Mary shook her head slowly. "No but what does that have to do with a solution to my problem?"

"The woman has two husbands.'

Mary's mouth dropped open. "Two?"

"Yes, and they are the law men in town. Respected

members of the community, all three of them, and yet they live as they please."

"How is that possible?" Mary felt a bloom of hope in her chest. If a woman was allowed to marry two men, then surely her right to take one wife was understandable.

"On account of Gold Sky not being your normal town, not even on the frontier." Alexi placed a hand on the pew in front of them and turned to face Mary fully. "This place is near magic in its ability to accept and encourage people to love and be themselves. I have never met a kinder group of individuals. All of us came here running, like I told you and it is here that we all found a reason to stop running."

Mary's eyes watered and she ducked her head, surprised at the sudden appearance of tears. "That sounds like a lovely thing to find," she husked out, wiping at the corner of her eyes.

"It can be yours as well, Minnie. You don't have to keep running." Alex reached out and placed a hand on hers.

"Even if I were able to marry a woman, what would that do for me? I am still without prospects for such a life and my mother is not of the same mind as Gold Sky. She would never allow it."

Alex patted her hand reassuringly. "That is where I come in. You already know me."

Mary's eyes widened in surprise. "But that means--"

"That you would marry *me*."

CHAPTER 5

"*M*arry...*you?*"

"Yes, me." Alex pressed a hand to her chest and smiled at her. "You already know me, so there will be no need to find a new prospect."

"But we, ah, we don't know one another," Mary whispered. She swallowed hard and continued on, "How are we to marry when we have only just met?"

"It would not be a true match. Not a marriage of love, but of one of necessity." Mary's heart sank at the clarification. Even if she had protested Alex's mention of a marriage to her it did not mean that the idea was wholly unappealing.

She gave Alex a tight smile. "Yes, of course. One of convenience but...what exactly is that convenience?"

"Getting you room to breathe, to be able to be yourself. I expect that you have been under your mother's heel for far too long now, hmm?" Alex looked at her with eyes that saw far too much and gave Mary an understanding smile.

"Yes, that's right. It hasn't been easy since papa passed away," she confessed and not for the first time since they had met took comfort in Alex's touch. She turned her hand so that they were able to interlace their fingers.

"But why would you marry me? If you do so then I get away from my mother, but what does that give you? Why would you tie yourself to someone you do not know for such a-a permanent arrangement such as marriage?"

"Marriage need only be as permanent as we see fit," Alex told her. "Remember what I said about the town. If we marry and separate, then they will allow it as surely as they will our nuptials."

"But why would you marry me, even if it can be undone?" Mary gave herself a pat on the back that her voice did not waver. It was not for her to feel rejection or a sense of disappointment that Alex, a woman offering to be her ally, a woman that she felt an attraction to and admitted she felt the same for Mary, would only be with her for a time. She shouldn't be fearful to lose Alex so quickly when they had only met that day, but already Mary felt a kinship to the woman she was reluctant to turn her back on.

"Someone once gave me a chance. A helping hand if you will." She squeezed Mary's hand and drew back. Mary had to dig her nails into her palm to stop herself from chasing the other woman's touch. "And I vowed to myself that I would give the same help I received if and when I was able to return the favor."

"And marrying me falls into that category?"

"Indeed it does," Alex told her. "Marrying me won't be so bad. I've got a good-sized house outside of town, you won't want for anything while you plan your future, you are welcome to stay and never go as well. It would be safe." She paused, and then added in a quieter voice, "You will not be a burden to me. Nor will the baby. I want you both to be safe and happy, Minnie."

Mary bit her lip. "Well and truly?"

"Yes, of course. If you were of a mind to stay in Gold Sky, then you would have a place with me for as long as you liked."

"I like the sound of that, but what do we do about my mother? She would never allow the marriage to take place. She doesn't-she doesn't understand any of this. She chooses to live in the world of her own creation and that does not allow for me marrying a woman. No matter how much I wish to."

Alex held up a finger and gave her an excited smile. "I have that all worked out! Just a minute and I'll show you." She rushed up from her seat and hurried towards the front of the church where she rummaged at a table. It was only when she held a newspaper in her hand and lifted it above her head with a whoop of triumph that she turned back towards Mary.

"I found it!"

"Found what?" Mary asked. She had to fight against the laugh that nearly escaped her when Alex whooped again and came forward waving the newspaper.

"I saw it here today and hid it to make sure that no one filched it for their own reasons. Pastor Bruce's sister has been on a rip about matchmaking and has taken every last advert for her own use."

"What advert?"

"This one!" Alex thrust the paper into Mary's hands early. "It is perfect for our scheme."

Mary looked the paper over, eyes moving over the small print to see that it was a page full of hopefuls advertising for spouses. The small neat script varied in its offerings, some looking for those good in the kitchen and inclined to have a family, others still searching for partners with loyal and warm dispositions, thrifty minded spenders, experienced horse workers, efficient farm hands, and more still seeking incomparable beauty, but each one thing above all: *a wife.*

"The mail order adverts?" Mary asked, looking up from the paper to see Alex watching her expectantly.

"Yes, my plan is simple. I post an advert in tomorrow's paper, one that is sure to interest your mother. You will respond, and our marriage will be set into motion immediately."

"But there's one thing I don't understand."

"What's that?"

Mary gestured to the paper with one hand and a tight smile. "All of these postings are by men looking for wives. How are we, ah, to disguise that you are a woman? My mother will no doubt ask after you in town and do her due diligence before she marries me off, even if it appears to be a godsend."

Alex grinned at her. "Now that you leave to me, Minnie. I'll put the word out in town that I am to be referred to solely by my name. Your mother need never know I am a woman. She'll be none the wiser until we are well and truly married but that will require you to do one important thing."

"What is it? I'll do anything." Mary leaned forward, fingers crumpling the periodical she clutched.

"Absolutely anything?" Alex asked. She came forward to stand in front of Mary and kneeled down in front of her so that the two of them were eye-to-eye. Mary's heart sped up at the close contact. It was nearly impossible not to notice the way the light hit Alex's brown eyes, they were a good deal more hazel than she had realized with flecks of green and amber mixed in with the rich brown color.

Mary's eyes moved over Alex's face, over and across the aquiline nose, the high cheekbones, along her sharp jawline and lush lips. Would they kiss on their wedding day? Or was such a thing unnecessary in a marriage such as theirs? In a marriage of convenience rather than passion. Even if they felt the inkling of a spark, the draw of attraction was not what put them together.

Kindness. Necessity.

Those were the things that would bind them together in matrimony, and it would all be done under the hand of deception to keep her mother from stopping it all and keeping Mary as she was---currently unsure of her own future, trapped in a cage of her own making, and all because she had not been strong enough to resist her mother's demands.

Alex did not know her, but she was helping her from a place of goodness. That kind of good did not come by often, and it had been extended to Mary fewer times than she could remember. She would not squander it. She would do her part to help their plan succeed.

"Yes, anything, I swear it." She reached forward and

caught Alex's hand. "I will not fail in what you ask of me, Alex."

Alex nodded at her. "I know you won't," she clasped Mary's hand with her own and smiled at her. "I know you will succeed, Minnie. Our plan hinges on one thing, and one thing only, and that is your ability to sneak out and marry me. We will have planned it carefully enough that your mother will know you have been married, and by the time she is aware I am a woman it will be too late. The town will accept us and she will not be able to force you back with her. She will have to leave you in peace, with me."

With me.

It made her stomach flutter with the stirrings of wanting, but Mary merely smiled and ignored the feelings. She had felt this sort of infatuation before, and she would not allow it to cloud her mind when it came to this. Not when Alex was doing her this sort of kindness. She would repay it with unfailing loyalty.

She had little to offer Alex, but she could be loyal, kind, and true.

Mary squeezed Alex's hand gently. "I will do it. I swear it."

WHEN MARY LEFT her meeting with Alex it was with a lightness in her heart that she hadn't felt in quite some time. She practically bounded down the chapel steps in search of her mother and Mr. Rutherford. It had been the unknowing, the vagueness of her future, that had caused her such worry and anxiety but knowing precisely what she was tasked with gave her the kind of purpose and direction she craved to create a sense of security.

She hadn't even realized how much she needed structure and certainty until Alex had blessed her with it tonight. Mary breathed a sigh of relief, a hand to her chest, and relished the feeling of being able to breath. She smiled and glanced around, surveying the festivities. Everyone seemed to be in high spirits, laughing and talking, dancing and eating their fill of treats. It was a beautiful night out just on the cusp of autumn, and Mary supposed there was no finer night for a fair. She was still smiling when Sarah James emerged from the crowd, Mr. Rutherford in tow and waved her down.

"Over here, dear!" Sarah James waved a hand cheerily. "Did you have a lovely time at the fair? We certainly did, didn't we, Bryan?"

Bryan?

Mary nearly raised an eyebrow at her mother's use of the man's first name, but she kept her features schooled into a picture of calmness.

"I did. It was quite good to spend the evening in the fresh air. I had an enjoyable evening, but I am finding I am quite tired now."

The sooner she was able to return to her room, the sooner she could go to sleep and get to the next morning's newspaper. The paper would contain Alex's advert and the first step of their plan to getting her out from under her mother's thumb. And so she smiled and nodded along as the couple told her of their night and asked of hers. She answered politely and calmly, playing the role of the dutiful and attentive daughter she knew was expected of her, and for once it did not feel forced, because finally there was an end in sight to it all.

That night Mary slept sounder than she had in months.

CHAPTER 6

$\mathcal{M}$ ary awoke the next morning before any in the boarding house did. There wasn't a soul stirring as she dressed in the dark. She took care in choosing her outfit, a yellow day dress she hadn't worn in quite some time but adored. It was plainer than her usual attire but was looser and easier on her body.

She sighed and put a hand to her stomach. If her mother had it her way her corset would be cinched impossibly tight and she never missed an opportunity to pull it as tight as she was able when she helped Mary dress. Waking before anyone else meant Mary would not have to suffer such attentions and her heart gladdened at that.

Today would be a wonderful day, she would begin her plan with Alex and manage to avoid having her breath stolen by her corset stays. The boning in her corset always left her skin tender, the stays digging painfully and making her gasp in a mixture of pain and relief once she was finally able to remove the garment.

When she was finished dressing Mary went to the window and glanced out to see the sky just beginning to turn pink with the dawn's first light. She put a hand up and leaned against the window frame with a sigh. Her plan was to spot the newspaper delivery and make her move to intercept it before any in the boarding house were the wiser. She would have to keep a keen eye and a sharp ear out as the boarding house staff were known to be early risers and were quick to take in the morning news for their own enjoyment. There was still some time to go before the morning's edition of the Gold Sky Gazette was printed and--

A figure appeared on the avenue and she leaned close to the window, pressing her nose to the glass trying to see who was out at this hour. Her eyes widened when she saw they had a satchel over their shoulder and were delivering newspapers to each business.

"Oh my stars," she breathed. It appeared the news was early today, and she had no complaints at the pleasant surprise. They were only two doors away now and she turned, rushing to her door as quietly as she was able. She had to get to the front door before anyone else and making a racket would do her no favors. Mary took in a deep calming breath. She held it in for a moment before letting it out slowly.

"Stay calm, stay calm. It's all going to happen. It will all work. You'll see," she whispered and took in another deep breath. Thank heavens she had the extra room in her dress to breathe comfortably. If her mother had done her up that morning she would have fainted by now. Slowly and carefully she unlocked her door and peered down the hallway. It was empty and quiet. The morning light showed her the faint outlines of the furniture and door-ways and she crept into the silent hallway with another furtive glance.

Mary winced with every creak and groan the floor-boards made beneath her feet but finally she was at the front door and not a moment too soon. She had just begun to peer through the curtained window when the silhouette of the newspaper delivery boy appeared at the bottom of the steps. He had hardly set a foot on the bottom step when Mary threw open the door and burst from the boarding house.

"Good morning!" she greeted and then clapped a hand over her mouth when she realized she had nearly shouted her hello. The newspaper boy yelped and fell onto his back in surprise.

"M-morning miss," he managed, shoving himself up onto his knees.

"I'm so sorry," Mary whispered, she glanced behind her, glad the house remained silent. "I didn't mean to scare you," she told him coming down the stairs and extending a hand. "Here, let me help you."

"Thank you, miss." He gave her a grateful if confused smile. "Eager for a bit of news, hmm?" he asked, rummaging through his satchel.

"Ah, yes, I am quite the voracious reader…" she clasped her hands and gave him a quick nod, her eyes on the paper he was fumbling for. Finally he handed it to her and Mary swore she had never held anything more precious.

This was her ticket out of her current folly. Her salva-tion and hopes for tomorrow. She cradled it close and laughed, the sound bubbling out of her before she could stop it. Not that she cared to.

"Well, have a good morning, miss." She opened her eyes to see the delivery boy giving her a confused look, but that didn't matter. He could think her as silly as he liked, because today everything changed. Mary waved happily at him and bid him goodbye before she turned and hurried back to her room. The journey back was significantly less fraught, and she was smiling ear-to-ear as she slipped back into her room and locked the door behind her.

"Let us see, let us see," she murmured, placing the newspaper onto the small window side table she normally did her needlepoint at. Opening the paper she frowned when she didn't immediately see the marriage adverts, but then here it was, right near the end and then bold as you please. Mary saw Alex's advert immediately.

The script was not as small as the rest, this was larger and bolder taking up nearly a quarter of the page and she laughed at how large it was.

Her mother would notice that the advert was no doubt pricier to place than the rest. Sarah James would quite enjoy that, as she would the contents of the marriage advert. There was no way anyone interested in securing a profitable match would dislike it.

Wealthy Investor Seeks Bride

Wealthy farmer seeks well educated lady as a wife. Farmer in possession of 2000 acre homestead with steady income. Young lady must be agreeable, adept at organizing and entertaining affluent business partners, and eager to start a family immediately. Looking for a speedy introduc-

tion with nuptials to follow. Young lady will be added to all banking and store accounts upon marriage.

Contact immediately through Gold Sky Gazette.

--Alex Pierce

Mary whistled in appreciation. She could almost see her mother's eager face when she presented her with the advert. Sarah James would practically demand she write her response immediately and hand deliver it to the newspaper office. There would be no ifs, ands, or buts, before the day was out Mary would have written to Alex and all with her mother's encouragement.

She turned when she heard a door open in the hallway. The house was slowly coming to life and overhead more telltale steps were heard as the other boarders awoke and began their morning ministrations.

Mary folded the newspaper and began to pace the length of the room. The advert was good, very good in fact, there was no way her mother wouldn't be interested in it but how would Mary broach the subject. Perhaps she would be able to convince her mother that the fair had ignited a need for her to be proactive in her search for a husband?

That could work. She had after all always tried to fulfill her role as a dutiful daughter for as long as she had been aware of the role. Sarah James might be suspicious of it but the fact that Alex's advert was nearly perfect would cause her mother to overlook any misgivings. She would be beside herself with excitement and that was where Mary would find her way to freedom.

A rap at the door alerted her to her mother's presence. Every morning the pair went to breakfast together. What her mother thought might happen to her between her room and the dining room Mary had no idea, but she opened the door with a sunny smile all the same.

"Good morning, mother."

"Good morning, dear. You look…" Sarah James leaned back and considered her daughter. "Well rested, for once."

"Ah, yes, the fair was just the thing I needed. Fresh air is good for the constitution," Mary told her mother conversationally. "Why, I even awoke early this morning and fetched the newspaper for a bit of light reading and you'll never guess what I happened upon."

"What was that?" Sarah James asked. They were now in the dining room and Mary handed her mother the mail order adverts with a hopeful smile.

"I think I found the solution to our problems. Look there at Alex Pierce's listing."

Sarah James took the paper with a delicate sniff and took her time unfolding it. "Hmmm," her mother hummed, glancing at it before she folded it once more and crossed to the made up breakfast table.

Mary stared after her in shock. Why was she not more interested? She had been so sure her mother would take the bait immediately. She hadn't counted *on this.*

"Are you not going to read it?" Mary asked nervously. She came forward haltingly and stopped when her mother pursed her lips glancing at her.

"Is it imperative that I read it before breakfast?"

"Well, no but there is a bit of exciting news to be had in there and if we dally, I'm worried we may miss out on-
-"

"The ink is hardly dry on the paper. I do not see how we can miss out on whatever news is to be had."

"Ah, yes, mother. You are quite right," she agreed with a fake smile. Mary took her seat and bit her lip, watching as her mother placed the newspaper on the table next to her plate. The boarding house staff came through serving them their breakfast of toast and tea. It was simple fare, but the women were on a budget after all and Sarah James had opted to save their remaining fortune for more important things like "letting your dresses out to hide our inconvenience."

Mary's breakfast tasted like ash in her mouth as she chewed. Normally their breakfasts were quiet, unless Sarah James was particularly motivated on a certain matter, which was more often than not as her mother was keen to be riled, but this morning her mother seemed content to drink her tea and eat her toast in silence with a smile on her face.

Mary considered her mother carefully. There was something odd about her. Her eyes widened when she realized her mother was smiling. It was not a wide sunny thing but more of a sly expression a satisfied cat might display and that had Mary paying close attention. Whenever her mother had such a look it meant there was a new scheme being planned.

But what?

Mary's breakfast went untouched, her hands stirring at her tea absentmindedly as she continued to watch for any sign of subterfuge, but she could find none. It was only when Sarah James had finished her toast and picked back up the newspaper that Mary's focus shifted. There would be plenty of time to figure out what her mother was up to but now she had a part to play. She worked to look natural and sipped at her tepid tea as her mother scanned the page, she could tell the exact moment she read Alex's advert, there was an audible snap of paper and a small gasp that demanded Mary look up at her mother.

"Why did you not tell me this was here?" Her mother snapped with an angry glare. "Do you know what time we have lost by you sitting there as if you have forgotten to speak?"

"But I did try to tell you," Mary protested. "You said--"

"Do not tell me what I said, you foolish girl. Now get up and get to your room at once! You must write this Mister Pierce at once. I want to look over what you write, in fact, I shall dictate your response. Fetch the paper and come back. Move, Mary for heaven's sake!"

Mary bobbed her head in a nod, scrambling towards the door and rushed for her desk. She kept a bundle of paper to write along with a pencil out of habit. She had once written to her friends, but it hadn't taken long for the rumors of her pregnancy to cause their letters to stop entirely. Associating with her was hardly fashionable. She didn't blame her old friends even if it did hurt her to realize they had abandoned her. She snatched the paper up, happy to have a reason to use it especially when that reason would get her closer to her goal of having a happy home and life.

She rushed back into the dining room and resumed her seat across from her mother. Sarah James was looking over the paper intently as if parsing out the words for clues. There was no hidden meaning or fancy language to consider in Alex's message and Mary nearly sighed at her mother's dramatics. Instead she smiled serenely at her and took up her pencil.

"What shall I write?" she asked.

"Begin as such," Sarah James said, head still bowed over the paper, "I am an educated, attractive and family oriented young lady. My name is Mary Sophia James and I have just arrived via San Antonio. You sound like a capable and diligent man. I find the terms of courtship agreeable and look forward to receiving your next correspondence. Forever yours, Mary Sophia."

Mary bit her lip at her mother's use of her full name. She never used it except for when her mother was determined to put on airs. She supposed responding to Alex was one such occasion, even if her letter bordered on a business transaction. There was none of the softness and infatuation she felt in her when she looked upon Alex. She was...soft when it came to the woman, drawn like a moth to a flame but this letter was clinical in approach and thin in substance.

No matter if it was not a letter professing adoration. Alex was guaranteed to reply no matter its contents. When she was finished she held it up with a wave.

"I'm all done."

"Do stop waving it about. You'll wrinkle the paper, Mary." Sarah James flicked a finger at the door looking for all the world as if she were a queen. "Now run it to the newspaper office immediately. If we are lucky no other respectable woman has seen it yet and we will have staked our claim first. We shall see how quickly the sir intends to marry and approach the courtship thusly."

She stood from her chair with a satisfied nod. "Now, I am off to do business."

"What kind of business?" Mary paused in the doorway and looked at her mother. "I mean, I didn't know we had any affairs in play here," she added when her other gave her a sharp look.

"If you must know, I am off to see Mr. Rutherford and I will do my best to find out if this Alex Pierce is truthful in their assertions or not. It always does well to do a bit of snooping when it comes to a man's fortune. No matter what they make claims to possess, the real truth is in the gossip. Remember that, Mary."

"Yes, mother," Mary chimed, nodding at her mother and making for the door once more. She was smiling when she left the boarding house. For all her mother's snooping she would only find what Alex had already asked the townspeople to say, and that heartened Mary some. There was nothing to worry over, she must simply keep her head and stick to their plan.

All would be well. She was sure of it.

"YOU SHALL NEVER BELIEVE what I heard today?" Sarah James entered her room with scarcely a knock. Mary sat up in her seat by the window, the needlepoint she had been working on clattering to the floor in surprise.

"Pardon?" she choked out, trying to calm her beating heart as her mother began to move about her room.

"Oh, Mary, do get your nerves under control. I have come with good tidings, my dear!" Her mother was practically skipping as she said this, and Mary knew Alex had done well in her advisement of the townspeople.

Her mother was not simply interested in the marriage advert, she was downright glowing. Ecstatic in her joy at the prospect of a wealthy savior.

"What good tidings might those be?" Mary asked, though she already knew.

"That your Mister Alex Pierce is a well and truly landed gentleman. He hails from New York, my dear. Old Money. Old money, indeed, and is even well connected enough to be in business with the Baptiste family."

Mary blinked at that. In business with Julian Baptiste? She hadn't known that, now had she?

"Oh, he is, is he?" she asked, and wondered why Alex had not told her. The connection was curious and for Mary served as a notable given Alex's offer to help her.

Julian Baptiste and his wife Violet were kind people, and if they were doing business of any sort with Alex it was just one more example to recommend her character. Mary frowned and wrung her hands together. She was marrying a good person with a good heart and selfless intentions, and yet, here she was scrambling to save herself behind her mother's back.

Selfish is how Mary felt, not selfless. However would they make their arrangement work when she was terrified of ruining it.

"Mary, where is your head at?" Her mother clapped her hands sharply, startling Mary from her thoughts. "Did you hear anything I said?"

She blushed and ducked her head. "No, mama. I'm sorry. I was, ah, it's just that--"

"Your mind was abuzz with all the advantages of marrying this desperate Mister Pierce, wasn't it?" Her mother tittered and wagged a finger at her with a wink. "You are your mother's daughter after all. I know that keen look in your eyes as well as any. I can't fault you for daydreaming, dear, but do keep on task with me, hmm?"

Mary swallowed and gave her mother a quick nod. "Yes, mama."

Sarah James gave her a satisfied smirk. Mary pursed her lips at the sunny expression on her mother's face. It was so unlike the cold and unfeeling smiles she was accustomed to, she had always reserved these warm expressions for her father, or really anyone she was of mind to use. The look gave Mary a nervous feeling and she looked away quickly.

"Now then, I have gone through the savings we have, and I estimate we will be able to purchase a wedding dress for you, but we must work quickly. It should be tasteful, yet simple. Nothing like the garment the Baptiste bride wore, but it will do, it will do," her mother sniffed, looking put out at the thought of anyone wearing a dress finer than she could provide. "I think a nice simple, modestly cut dress trimmed in lace will suffice, don't you?"

Mary nodded. She didn't care if she had to wear burlap and denim to the chapel so long as she was able to marry Alex.

"Yes, understated, and ah, frugal. Mister Pierce seems to be a man inclined to value a frugal woman. It can be seen as an asset rather than a shortcoming," Mary said, and her mother lit up with an excited clap of her hands.

"That is right! Too true, Mary, too true. Now you are thinking, and to think I lamented sending you to all the fine schools we could. It seems now you are earning back every penny of your tuition. We will make it seem as if it were a choice and not a matter of circumstance, because I do have another glad tiding to share with you, my dear."

Mary fought against the flutter of panic in her chest. She hated it when her mother brought news to her, it was never pleasant, at least never for Mary. As Sarah James's daughter she had never been in a position that her mother thought her useful or valuable, she had always been ordered to do this or that without niceties or pleasantries.

But now here was *that smile.* Mary shifted uncomfortably and forced her attention on her mother.

"What is it?" she asked. "What happy news do you have?"

Her mother shot her a coquettish smile. "You didn't think this happy season was all about you, now did you? Your mother has her own bit of happiness to share as well."

"No, I didn't think it was--"

"Mister Rutherford has asked to marry me!" Her mother announced, throwing her arms out wide. She crossed the room to grasp her daughter's hands excitedly. "We will announce a double wedding and the whole affair shall be quite fetching."

"A double wedding?" Mary felt faint at the announcement. She turned away and looked back out the window. All of her happiness at escaping this, of getting out from under her mother's thumb for her own life suddenly felt precarious. A double wedding meant that her wedding was not her own, it was her mother's. Sarah James would not be out of her life or even a safe distance away, she would be right beside her and Mary could not take the thought.

"But why would we do such a thing?" she asked, her voice coming out higher than she anticipated. She winced and twisted her fingers in her skirts knowing that her mother would most assuredly catch the misstep.

"And why would we not?" Her mother asked from behind her, Mary wrapped her arms around herself hearing the approaching footsteps. "Such a thing is precisely what we need to make this town our home for good."

"But I thought you meant to move on after I was married?" She turned then to face her mother. "You have been pushing me ever forward on the stipulation that it would free you to do as you pleased. I thought you meant to move to New York City when I was married off?"

Sarah James waved a hand. "Yes, that was the plan, but now things have changed. Why would I leave, even for a city so grand as New York, when I have Mister Rutherford wanting me for a wife?"

"And what do you know of the man? Why would he wish to be married so quickly?"

"Why?" Sarah James shook her head at her daughter. "As a man of his influence, he requires a skilled lady in his home when it comes to matters of business and entertaining. As you know, I was an asset to your father in his business dealings. The pair of us made a wonderful team. Everyone in San Antonio knew that, now didn't they, dear?" Mary didn't miss the inflection her mother took

65

on at the end, or the meaningful look she gave her daughter.

Sarah James was skilled at playing hostess but only with a seasoned staff on hand. The woman had little understanding of business, much more inclined to pursuing the newest fashion periodicals than sitting with her husband as he pored over new business contracts. Mary had sat with her father and listened to him, tried to soak in the knowledge he gave her.

"Pay me mind and it will secure your future one-day, darling Minnie. You have a sharp mind."

But her mother on the other hand had thought them boring and stuffy, waving the pair of them off as she left for another social engagement. Mary hadn't minded her mother's absence then; her father was pleasant enough company and there had always been a snifter of brandy when they spent time together.

Mary raised an eyebrow at her mother. "You are aiming to give Mister Rutherford business help?"

"Yes, of course. Like any good wife and partner, and as I said, I had done so for years with your father, now isn't that right?" This time there was no mistaking her mother's sharp tone. Mary was to fall in line and support her mother's story and immediately so.

"Ah, yes, yes of course. You always did help Papa when there were important decisions to be made," Mary acquiesced.

Sarah James nodded approvingly at her. "Perfect, darling I knew it was just your memory, the frontier does make you so forgetful, now isn't that right?"

Mary nodded. "Yes, of course, you're right."

"Now then, as I was saying on the matter of the double wedding. We can plan it post haste and spare no expense. I already have my mind set on a new dress, I am thinking perhaps velvet, there are so many becoming designs as of late for a woman of my age. I shall head to the nearest modiste at once for a fitting. The food will also be top quality as well, we must make sure Mister Rutherford understands we are women of means and will settle for nothing less if he hopes to keep your Mama close."

Mary furrowed her brow. "But I thought-didn't you say that we must be frugal with our spending? And my simple dress?" she asked, shocked by her mother's sudden change in tack. "I thought--"

"Mister Pierce will be able to pay for it all," Sarah James interrupted.

Mary's eyes widened at her mother's words. "What?"

"Your soon to be husband will, of course, pay for the entire thing." Her mother gave her a quizzical look. "You did write him back haven't you?"

"Yes, of course, but what do you mean he will pay for it? Why would he do that?"

"To please his new family."

Mary gaped at her mother. "But we have not even received his response yet. For all we know he has chosen another woman to respond to. How can you already be so sure that he has chosen us?"

"Because, I, in my infinite wisdom, have taken care of it. When I went asking after him, I made sure the newspaper office would not forward on any other responses. Only yours has made it through to the young man."

"How did you manage that?"

"It was quite simple really. The delightful young woman that ruins the office came up with the idea all on her own. Have you met her? Rosemary was her name. I could not think of a more delightful woman in all of Gold Sky. She and I are of quite the same mind, you know? I must introduce you to her at once. We will have her over once you're all settled and we are out of these horrid rooms." She looked around her with a disgusted sniff.

Mary didn't think the boarding house was the height of comfort, but it was nice enough. Nothing horrid about them, but she kept her mouth shut and nodded stiffly. She knew that it was all arranged between her and Alex beforehand and for that she was happy. If it had not been, she did not know if she would have been able to carry on otherwise. The thought of an unsuspecting groom falling prey to her mother's mechanisms had her stomach roiling---she paused at that.

Mister Rutherford.

The man seemed affable enough. He had certainly gotten her the time alone she had so desperately needed and wanted. Mary had no reason to think poorly of him, and her mother was pulling the wool right over his eyes proclaiming that she was in possession of a head for business. The man would be marrying a stranger.

"Now then, I am off to the modiste to get my measurements taken. Come along as well, dear. We can have them begin your dress and see if there has been a new letter for you as well." Sarah James strode towards the door. "Let's be off then."

Mary followed behind on numb feet. She could not think of Mister Rutherford or what would happen when he found out the truth. The most important thing now was to take care that she kept to her plans with Alex. Whatever actions her mother chose now would not, and could not affect her, even if it meant abandoning Mister Rutherford to her mother's designs.

CHAPTER 7

*M*ary slipped from the dress shop with a barely restrained sigh. It had been a trying morning at her mother's side. She glanced towards the shop windows and shook her head when she caught sight of her mother standing before a selection of materials--velvet and silk. Mary did not miss how her mother had chosen only the most sumptuous and expensive fabrics for herself while her daughter's dress was to be made of a sturdy and plain cotton trimmed with a simple lace.

The dress Mary would wear could double as a Sunday dress, and it was far more suited to her taste than anything her mother would choose for herself. Her mother's decision to use their meager wealth on herself was a blessing as Mary would now be able to wear her wedding dress happily. She had only played ignorant when it came to her mother's allocation of their resources. It had all been too convenient that Mary was to wear the simple dress while her mother chose only the most luxurious trappings for herself.

It was all just as well. Mary saw the marriage as simply a means to an end, and not a happy occasion, she reminded herself. The flutter in her heart told her otherwise, as did the attraction she felt for Alex. Mary found it difficult not to think the woman beautiful, smart and strong, the mix of it intoxicating to her in a way that left her wanting more.

She sighed, shaking her head at the whole predicament and continued on towards the newspaper office. She had been given leave to check with Miss Rosemary in regard to a reply from 'Mister Pierce.' She bit her lip when the newspaper windows came into sight. Would she have to pretend with this Miss Rosemary?

Her mother had described the woman as being like-minded. The prospect of a woman akin to her mother made her frown, but she wiped the expression from her face as she came to the front door. She could not let her feelings be revealed, not this close to the goal she had for herself. Taking in a deep breath Mary reached out and opened the door.

"Hello?" she called out upon entering the office. She glanced around the office noting the desks in a row, the stacks of paperwork and the sight of a printing press at the far end of the room greeted her. It was exactly the same as when she had visited that morning, except that instead of bustling activity and writers furiously working, the room was empty and silent. She hesitated, wondering if she should wait in the office or if she should return.

Mary continued forward and stopped in front of the

press. She hadn't been able to get close to it earlier when it had been hard at work printing that afternoon's edition. She moved closer to it now, never having seen one up close and leaned forward looking at the machine in earnest.

"Lovely machine, isn't it?" A voice asked, startling her, and Mary muffled a curse as she spun around to see a blonde woman striding towards her. The woman was lovely, she wore a gorgeous blue wool dress lined with pearl buttons and a pale pink lace at the cuffs and bustle. Her hair was swept up from her face, a pearl hair comb held her hair in place though the fine accessory shared its place with a pencil tucked behind her ear.

"You must be Mary! How are you dear? My name is Rosemary."

"Ah, I'm well, but how do you know who I am?" Mary forced herself to stand where she was and not shrink away from a woman she knew to be like her mother.

"Alex stopped by and informed me that a Titian haired beauty would be coming my way," the woman replied with a wink. "I'm terribly sorry that I missed you this morning, dear. I heard about you from the other reporters though and they had much to say about you."

"They did?"

"Oh yes, my dear. They said you were lovely! Now your mother on the other hand." Rosemary's lips pulled down in a frown. "That woman is...interesting to say the least. Spirited and all that."

Mary laughed. "Yes, that is one way of putting it. You spoke with her earlier?"

"I did, I did. I also spoke to Alex and she informed me

of your little arrangement. Not to worry, I am firmly in support of your decision. I must say that I entirely understand your decision to, ah, make your own way in the world."

'You do?" she asked in surprise.

"Oh, yes, your mother is...a woman with ideas that serve only herself. You need not fear me. I am on your and Alex's side. Please do not be scared." Miss Rosemary held out a hand to her and gave her a reassuring smile. "I know it's frightful for you right now, but I am not the kind of woman I led your mother to believe."

Mary relaxed and let out a nervous laugh. "Oh, I don't mean to look scared it's just that she said you were like her and I didn't know what to think."

"Come and sit for a moment? I was just making a cup of tea. I can pour you one if you like."

"That would be lovely. I've been at the dress shop all morning and I could use a cup of tea to calm myself."

"Already fitting you for a dress, is she?" Rosemary asked, leading Mary over to a side table where a steaming pot of tea sat. She poured them each a cup and gestured towards one of the chairs at the table. "Please sit. You must be exhausted; she was in quite a state of excitement this morning asking after Alex's holdings."

"Thank you." Mary sank into the seat with a grateful sigh and took the cup from Rosemary. She sipped at her tea for a moment and Rosemary settled in across from her, waiting for her to speak. "Yes, she was very excited this morning. She's even begun an order for herself."

"Herself?" Miss Rosemary raised an eyebrow.

"Yes, she means to marry one of the newly arrived

bankers. It will be a double wedding," Mary informed her.

"Oh no."

"Oh yes." Mary gave her a wry smile and took another sip of her tea. "Although, I have a plan to get away from that. I cannot be married with my mother beside me, you see."

Miss Rosemary nodded. "I understand entirely. The whole thing seems over the top."

"Such is my mother's way."

"You poor dear. I am so glad you met Alex the way that you did. She is beside herself with excitement over you and your coming nuptials."

"She is?" Mary asked in surprise. She leaned forward eagerly for more news. "How do you mean?" She had thought this was all business and strictly from the kindness of Alex's giving heart, not an event the woman would be excited over.

"Well, how can she not be excited to get a bride and a baby in such short order."

Mary jerked in surprise. "You know about the baby?"

"Yes, I do, but I have not told a soul. Even if I did it would not matter here. Babies are a blessing on the frontier, and we greet each of them with joy and happiness. You will not be looked down upon for it."

Mary felt like the floor had opened up beneath her, the curious sense of falling overtaking her suddenly. How had she been living for months with her mother telling her how precarious her life was, how suddenly she was on borrowed time and that once her condition became apparent no one of good standing would want her near.

And here Miss Rosemary was telling her that life in

Gold Sky offered something entirely different for her and her child.

They need not run and hide the birth, nor her method of conception. A baby would be welcomed, not reviled.

A shuddering breath escaped her at the news and she nearly laughed. Instead she sank back in her chair with a nod at Rosemary. "That's very kind of you to say," she whispered.

"I just cannot wait for the wedding! It will be a lovely affair, you'll see. The town of Gold Sky knows how to care for its own and that is what you are now." The other woman beamed at her and gave her hand a squeeze. Mary blinked back tears and smiled at her.

"That's so kind of you to say. Thank you." Her voice was soft, and she had to look away, lest she burst into tears. She had been without an anchor since her father passed away but now here was a place that she could tether herself to and find peace. "Everyone here has been so kind to me even after my deplorable behavior when first arriving."

Miss Rosemary reached across the table and put a hand over hers. "We all do things we are not proud of, dear. That is not the summation of your character but only a look at who you were in that moment. You do not have to let it define you if you do not wish it to."

"I know that but…" Mary swallowed hard and shook her head. "It's difficult to understand it. I have been scared for so long, and anxious as well. I do not know how to set things right, not truly."

"You are speaking of how you treated someone?"

"Yes, Violet Shield, well, now Baptiste. I was silent on

75

matters when I should have spoken out. She did not deserve the treatment she suffered from my mother or myself. Not over a man, and to be truthful not over anything. It was terrible how she was nearly ruined."

"Ah, *that.*" Miss Rosemary nodded and then said, "Do you know what I have learned from such situations?"

"No, what?"

"That when you treat a person badly, it is not because of what they have done but what is wrong in here," She tapped a finger against her chest. "And that once you realize that, you can truly make amends."

"And how do I make amends?"

"You ask for forgiveness of course, dear. Plain and simple. You are not the only one to ever commit such an act and you shall not be the last. I myself was a doer of such animosity."

Mary looked at her in surprise. "You? But you're so kind and warm."

"People can be both," Rosemary replied with a little shrug and sipped her tea. "People have the capacity for great kindness and mercy as well as ugliness. It depends on our hearts and where they are in that moment. I have chosen to fix mine and in doing so have been able to rectify my actions."

"But *how?*"

"I apologized."

"That's it?"

Miss Rosemary smiled at her. "I sincerely and honestly apologized. I made no excuses and asked for forgiveness. I was lucky to be given that grace by those I wronged. I cherish them and their friendships to this day."

Mary chewed on her bottom lip in consideration. "I must apologize to Violet at once."

"It would do you a world of good, dear."

She pushed away from the table and nodded, already making for the door. "You are right, I will find her and lay my heart bare."

"But do not forget your letter from our dear Alex!" Miss Rosemary called out, holding a letter above her head. "Your mother will be expecting you to return with it in hand."

"Oh! You're right!" Mary rushed back to grab the letter but not before she bent low and hugged Rosemary tightly. "Thank you for your advice and for listening to me. You have been a godsend to me. I will never forget it."

Rosemary hugged her back. "My pleasure, Mary. And welcome to Gold Sky."

MARY SAT at her writing desk that night and stared at the letter with a considerate look. She had thought the letter might be full of nothing, or at the very least a play at a fake correspondence should her mother look it over, but it was not.

The letter was well and truly *written*. It was a look into Alex's mind and heart. She asked her what her favorite foods were, how she came to like the Montana Territory, and what she thought she might like to do when this was all over.

"What does your future look like? Your perfect day? Tell me. Mine consists of a late rise, breakfast of a rasher of bacon and a

strawberry shortcake piled high with summer sweet strawberries."

Mary bit her lip, fingers twitching against the paper beneath her hands. *Summer sweet.* The words conjured thoughts of Alex's full lips. The woman's lips were plump, pink, and ripe for the taking. She would no doubt taste of summer sweet, of sunshine and the promise of a better tomorrow.

Of course she loved strawberries when she was as ripe for the picking as any fresh picked berry.

Mary's fingers tightened on the pencil she held, and she took out another piece of paper. She would tell Mary what her perfect day was. That it would be all gentle mornings with a cup of warm tea and all the biscuits and cake they both could eat, and books, there would, of course be books. What little solace Mary had found in the last few months had been in the pages of a good book.

Mary's perfect day would be the one that she chose. It didn't matter what she did, or what she ate. It mattered not where she was, so long as she chose it. She touched her pencil to paper and began to write.

CHAPTER 8

"It needs to be nipped in at the waist more. I look far too matronly for my liking." Sarah James turned this way and that in the dress shop mirror with a frown. "And for god sake do something about the lace at the back. It looks bedraggled and cheaply done."

Mary raised her eyes from the letter she was reading from Alex to see that her mother had sent the modiste scampering about with her assistant once more. They had been in the shop for nearly three hours and Sarah James had yet to exhaust her seemingly never-ending list of complaints and criticisms concerning her wedding attire.

Mary's own dress had been sorted out. The simple dress was easily made and already wrapped in paper and ready for Mary's big day. It was a day that had yet to be decided on, or at least formally, even though she told her mother differently. It had taken a few letters over so many days for Sarah James to tire of reading over their correspondence. It had been two days since her mother had taken any interest in Mary's letters--her daughters' words of assurance more than enough to accord with Sarah James's plans.

The distraction of her mother's wedding was a blessing in disguise as it wholly kept Sarah James's attention. Mary winced when her mother began berating the staff once more, and before she could stop herself, she stood and quickly tucked the letter away in her glove.

"Mama, I think the staff here," she gave both women a kind smile, "have done an exceptional job and that perhaps a kind word of acknowledgement would encourage them to continue in their efforts."

Sarah James's mouth fell open at her daughter's rebuff. She drew herself up to her full height and gave her a frosty glare. "Isn't there something you need to see to, dear?"

"No, there's nothing at all and in fact--"

"I believe there is. You have your dress in hand, do you not? Take it and leave on your errands."

Mary glanced at the two women who were watching them with interest. It was evident her mother wanted her out of the shop and seeing as she was right on all accounts there was no reason for Mary to stay. She sighed and gave her mother a curt nod.

"All right, mama. I will see you when you are done with your fitting." She gave both women an apologetic smile. "Thank you for your work. It is lovely, and I am so happy to wear this on my wedding day." She held up her dress and wished she could say more but her mother would surely make her pay for even one more word.

"Ah, good day, ladies... mama." She nodded at them all and, under the heavy weight of her mother's glare, Mary made a quick exit from the shop, dress tucked close to her.

She let out a sigh once the door was shut behind her. She wished she could do more than a gentle rebuff, but she knew any more would draw her mother's attention back to her plans and she could not have that. Mary set off down the boardwalk, but her steps faltered when she realized she hadn't the first clue where she was meant to go. She had never previously been allowed any more than two hours' free time without her mother keeping watch over her and now she was presented with a seemingly free day.

She could do anything.

However, that much freedom was daunting. What ever would she do with all of it? Mary bit her lip and began to walk once more, her body swinging into motion. Perhaps a treat to celebrate?

Her stomach growled and Mary sighed, patting a hand to her belly and then letting it rest there. Her mother had been keeping a close eye on every morsel she ate on account of "keeping her figure in hand" and Mary was starved. She was often starving, and she hated it. Once she was free of her mother, she would never allow herself or her baby to be in such a predicament again.

"I am sorry, little one," she murmured with a wince. Her hand at her stomach still, she rubbed the very slight curve, though she could scarcely feel the tender touch through the barriers of her corset and day dress. She frowned, wondering if her baby knew she was doing her utmost to offer comfort. Most likely not. Though she hadn't a clue what a baby did and did not know at this stage of her pregnancy.

Mary would get something to eat, for the both of them, and enjoy it in the fresh summer air. She did have a bit of pocket money saved away. She turned the corner already knowing that she wanted to make a stop at Lily's Cafe for one of the freshly baked treats the woman served there. Her steps quickened, the thought of baked sweets on her tongue working as adequate motivation for her trip. So distracted Mary was that she didn't see Alex until the pair were practically colliding.

"I'm so sorry!" Mary held out her hands and apologized with a worried frown. "My mind was elsewhere, and I wasn't, ah, I was just not looking where I was going."

"It's no trouble," Alex replied, reaching out to steady Mary where she swayed. "I'm sturdy. It'll take more than a run in with you to knock me down, Minnie."

Mary's heart warmed at the term of endearment. Every time she heard it slip from Alex's mouth she was heartened. She could be Minnie with the other woman, a precious gift indeed. She gave Alex a warm smile.

"I reckon you are right on that account. I was just on my way to Mrs. Lily's Cafe for a treat. Would you care to join me?"

"I would love nothing more." Alex gestured towards the cafe with a grin and a wink. "Lead the way, fair lady."

"I told you. I'm no lady."

"And I told you," Alex fell in step beside her, hands clasped behind her back as she walked with Mary, "that I have a nose for ladies, and you are indeed, one of the first order. A high-class lady."

Mary scoffed but she would be lying if she did not admit to preening a bit at the words. Alex had a way of making her want to simper and blush. It should have made her sigh at herself but instead, Mary quite enjoyed the feeling of careless frivolity.

Alex bounded up the steps ahead of Mary and opened the cafe door with a flourish. "After you, my lady."

Mary's cheeks warmed but she stepped inside all the same. The pair made their way to the pastry counter and Mary surveyed the items it held. There were pies, and cookies, muffins and even small cakes that looked heavenly. She hesitated looking at the cakes, remembering Alex's letter on the perfect breakfast.

"Strawberry shortcake," Mary said, tapping a finger against the glass.

"What was that?" Alex gave her a quizzical look and stepped closer. The step brought them into close proximity, elbows brushing against the other, the smell of soap and leather filling Mary's nose. She sniffed again and smiled when she realized it was Alex. Of course, the other woman would smell enticing in addition to looking as much.

"Your favorite dessert," Mary said gesturing towards the cakes once her brain had cleared enough for her to speak. She licked her lips and fixed her eyes on the dessert rather than meet Alex's eyes. All it would take was one glance into the pair of warm brown eyes for her to do something truly rash.

Although, once a woman agreed to marry another, Mary wasn't sure what other rash decision was left for her to make.

Alex beamed at her. "You remembered!"

"Of course, your letters are my favorite indulgence."

This time it was Alex who blushed. "And yours mine, Minnie. They brighten my day with each and every line."

Mary's heart skipped a beat. Her pulse hammered in her throat and she let out a nervous titter. "That's kind of you to say," she murmured.

"Not a kindness when it is the truth, Minnie."

Mary ducked her head, a smile tugging at the corner of her lips. She might have said more but Mrs. Lily was there and smiling at them with a notepad in hand.

"What would you like today, ladies?"

"Oh, well I'm not sure on that account." Alex gave Mary a sidelong look. "Unless you have made your mind up?"

"I have," Mary said with a nod. "The shortcakes. I would like all the shortcakes."

"All of them? How splendid. I'll just box these up for you. That will be two dollars."

"Thank you!" Mary was already fishing in her small reticule for her spending money when Alex put a hand on her arm.

"Minnie, that's entirely too much to spend on desserts. Allow me to--"

"No, no, this is my treat. You love them so." She handed the money to Mrs. Lily who was now looking at the women with a curious smile.

"Thank you, I'll just be a moment getting your change there, dear." She turned to leave the couple, who in Mrs. Lily's estimation, seemed to be in need of just the right amount of alone time. Who knew what wondrous things might happen in a moment of silence?

"But what are we to do with all these cakes?" Alex wanted to know.

Mary gave a little shrug. "Eat them? Give them away? Whatever you choose, I suppose."

"Oh, anything?"

"Yes, anything. But why are you giving me such a funny look?"

"Because, I have had the most splendid idea, Minnie. One worthy of the amount of cakes you just purchased."

"And what would that be?" Minnie asked, her heart pounding. She had no clue what Alex was about to propose but she did know one thing with certainty. Whatever it was, Mary would agree, and wholeheartedly so.

"Why, a wedding, of course."

"A wedding but for whom?" Mary looked around the cafe wondering if the bride and groom were in the establishment.

"Yes, a wedding. What else is a wealth of shortcake best used for, other than weddings? And only the most special of weddings, my dear, Minnie."

"And what wedding would that be?" Minnie asked, half distracted as she accepted the money Mrs. Lily was handing back to her.

"Why ours, of course."

Mary dropped the coins, but not the cakes, and for that she would always be grateful.

THE PAST HALF hour of Mary's life had been nothing short of a frenzy.

No, a flurry of activity.

Was a flurry more disorienting than a frenzy? Mary pursed her lips and thought it over for a moment before she gave herself a mental shake. She couldn't dither now, not when she had to get to the chapel. She smoothed her hands over the plain dress she wore.

When Alex had sprung her plan on her, Mary had balked at the idea of them marrying on such short notice.

"We can't," she whispered, trying to keep her voice low, but Mrs. Lily was grinning ear-to-ear as she had already heard Alex's words. The older woman merely tipped her head at them before she busied herself wiping down a nonexistent spot at the far end of the pristine counter. Mary was thankful for the bit of privacy.

"Why not?"

"Because, well, because marriages are not so hastily done!"

"But we have already planned to wed, what was it?" Alex tilted her head back and began to count on her fingers, "two, no three days prior. I would say that we have planned as much as any frontier arranged marriage."

Mary's throat tightened. Arranged marriage. She did not like to think of it as such, but Alex was right. She paused and cleared away the lump growing there.

"We would require more than cakes to marry, Alex."

"Yes, there is a dress to think of but what you are wearing currently is fine as anything, so long as you are in it." She winked at Mary, making her flush, and continued on merrily. "There is the matter of a pastor, but

I have first-hand knowledge that Pastor Bruce is hard at work cleaning the pews today and wouldn't mind the break."

"And what about a witness?" Mary asked, she looked down at the package still tucked under her arm and realized she had her wedding dress with her. Perhaps they did not lack as much as she thought to marry so suddenly.

Alex waved a hand. "That is easily done. I have friends all over town. Any one of them would be more than happy to stand in for us if I ask. There is nothing holding us from marrying."

Mary held up her package. "I have my dress here. I was just at a fitting. My mother is there now."

Alex raised an eyebrow at her and leaned an elbow against the counter. "Then we are free to make your escape, are we not?"

"We are," Mary said and chewed on her bottom lip with a furrowed brow. "But then what will we do?"

"Why, move your things to my home. Begin your new life in Gold Sky! But we can wait if you are unsure...or if you prefer to tell your mother?"

Mary shook her head and laughed. "No, no. The plan was never to tell her. She wouldn't allow us to go through with it. I, ah, I just hadn't thought the opportunity would present itself so quickly or easily. It's been such a trying time. It seemed the days leading up to our marriage would be more of the same."

"I understand, but life need not always be difficult. There are moments of joy, peace, and ease. We can have that now, but only if you are ready. I don't mean to rush you. The thought of all those shortcakes excited me." Alex reached out and touched her arm and Mary was undone by that gentle brush of fingers.

Alex was strong and wild, but the woman was also gentle, soft and sweet.

Mary wanted more *sweet* in her life.

The pair had left the cafe arm-in-arm, heads bent close as they worked out the particulars of conveying Mary's meager belongings to Alex's home, a respectable homestead on plenty of acreage containing everything a family would need to thrive. There was a barn, stables, a paddock, and chicken coops to occupy Mary, though she hadn't the first clue of what to do with the livestock that lived within each. Never the matter, she would figure it all out in the days to come. What mattered now was the wedding, the wedding her mother must not know about until it was far too late.

She moved to the window and peeked out nervously. She stood in the boarding house she had once been thrown out of. Ms. Alice Hill had taken her back with little fuss and a bemused smile when she opened the door at Alex's knock.

"Well, look what the cat drug in," she mused, giving Mary a once over before turning to Alex. "You always did have a weakness for a damsel-in-distress."

Mary bit her tongue while Alex rolled her eyes. "I like what I like. She needs a place to ready for the wedding. Will you help us, Alice?"

The other woman turned her shrewd eyes on Mary then and considered her. The once-over did nothing to calm Mary's already buzzing nerves. She knew what Ms. Alice Hill was remembering. Her abhorrent behavior the last time Mary had been a guest of hers and she stepped forward from Alex then with an apologetic nod.

"I would not blame you if you chose not to help us now. When I was last a guest, I was...weak. I allowed my mother to say what she wanted without correction. I did not conduct myself in a manner befitting anyone decent, and I am deeply sorry for it. I apologize to you, and I will apologize to Ms. Violet when I see her again. The last time I saw her was very brief, you see."

Ms. Alice Hill hummed. "It was. You were in and out of here so fast I scarcely realized it, though I do know why."

"Oh, yes, that."

"That was a big deal indeed. You helped those two lovesick idiots see the truth even as your mother pushed you towards Julian. Why did you help them?"

"Because they were in love at first sight, I expect. Perfect for the other. I had to act," Mary said. It was true. She had not missed the lingering looks between Violet and Julian. It had been tender to see, even with her mother's meddling.

"Yes, you did. I am glad you did. It showed me you are not your mother's daughter." Ms. Hill opened the door wider and gestured for Mary to enter. "Come on inside then. I suspect you won't have much in the way of motherly support on such a big day."

"No," Mary shook her head, stepping inside and following behind Ms. Hill. "I won't."

Ms. Hill had whisked her away then with a tut and a warm smile. She'd helped Mary dress for the wedding and had even done her hair up real nice with a sprig of flowers she had plucked from the vase in the room. It was a spray of wildflowers, their pretty yellow color making Mary think of sunshine and, of course, Alex. The woman was in her every thought as of late, making her feel excited and out of sorts, but in the very best way.

At least Mary had managed to find a partner that made her feel thus, even if their marriage was an arranged affair. She sighed and let the curtains go, stepping back from the window. She had been keeping a careful vigil for her mother's familiar form but so far the elder James had not been spotted.

That was either a blessing or a curse. She uttered a silent prayer to the modiste working with her mother. The woman would need a good bit of relaxation that evening to recover from the ordeal. Her nerves must be shot by now, but Mary was glad for the distraction, without it their plan would not be possible. She turned at a knock at the door.

"Yes?" she called, hurrying over.

"Are you ready?" Ms. Hill asked, opening the door and sailing in without so much as a step of hesitation. She nodded in approval at Mary's appearance. "Oh, you are a lovely bride indeed. Alex is a very lucky woman."

Mary shook her head. "No, it is I who is lucky."

"Well, then let's call it even and declare the pair of you lucky, hmm?"

"I quite like the sound of that."

"Perfect. Now come with me. We haven't much time. I was just sent word that your mother is finishing at the dressmaker. We must make haste now. Step lively, step lively!" Ms. Hill ushered her towards the door with a wave of her hands.

Mary swallowed hard, her heart pounding at the news. "Oh, dear, oh dear."

"Hush, she won't catch you before the deed is done. Gold Sky is on the case and getting in her way. She'll scarcely make it to the square by the time you say, 'I do' and by then it will be far too late, especially with the whole town knowing."

"The whole town?" Mary's feet turned to stone and she nearly tripped. "How will the whole town know?" she asked.

Ms. Hill was in front of her now and at the front door. She turned to look at Mary over her shoulder and grinned. "Why because they will all be in attendance. And you cannot deny or take back what an entire town has seen with their own eyes," she said and threw the door open with a flourish. "See?"

"W-what?" Mary squeaked. No other sound was possible when faced with what appeared to be the entirety of Gold Sky standing at the steps of the boarding house. She swallowed nervously when several of them waved to her or called out greetings of good tidings.

"What do you mean what? Look and see for yourself," Ms. Hill reached out and pulled her forward gently. "When there is a happy occasion, we all turn out to greet it together. Your wedding to Alex will bring so much happiness. She's a good woman with a big heart, and you, I am seeing, are as well. You must be, if Alex chose you for her bride."

"Oh, but it's all just a favor really, it isn't--"

"No time for words, Mary. You'll be late to your own wedding." Ms. Hill looped her arm with hers and guided her forward. "Make way, make way, the bride is coming!"

The crowd parted and Mary swore she had never seen so many smiles. All of them genuine and true. She had expected little happiness in her marriage and here she was being presented with buckets of it, and she hadn't even laid eyes on Alex. She nearly pinched herself to see if she were daydreaming, but she didn't dare chance waking from a dream as beautiful as this. Her walk across the town square and up the steps of the chapel happened in a flash and then the chapel doors were creaking open to reveal still more happy folk.

The entire town in attendance. For her wedding.

Mary's eyes prickled and she sniffled back the tears. Ms. Hill patted her shoulder comfortingly and then stepped away from her. "Best you continue on your own, Mary."

She nodded, knowing Ms. Hill was right and looked up the aisle to see Alex waiting for her. Mary felt the air punch from her lungs at the sight. Alex's golden hair was combed neatly, and she was wearing a fine suit made of tawny material. Mary was sure the suit would perfectly set off the woman's warm eyes and she smiled, taking her first step towards her soon-to-be wife.

On shaky legs Mary made her way up the aisle and to Alex who was looking at her as if she were the most important person in the world. Mary had not had such a tender expression aimed her way since her father's passing and she hurried towards it without even a hint of the grace and poise she should have displayed after years of finishing school.

Airs and refinement had no place here. Not when her heart was beating wildly in her chest, not when Mary felt she could scarcely breathe without fainting. She had to be at Alex's side. She must, and so she arrived with a breathy laugh and sweaty palms beside the blonde.

"You look beautiful," Alex whispered, leaning close to Mary.

"You look dashing," Mary offered in reply. Alex said nothing but the glow of pleasure across her features was unmistakable and Mary smiled knowing she had put it there. She would do her best to keep it so.

"Hello, you two." The man in front of them smiled kindly. "I am Pastor Bruce, but you know that already, hmm?" Mary nodded, recognizing the man from her Sundays in church. He was a warm man who spoke frankly, and she quite enjoyed his sermons, far more than she had any in quite some time. It cheered her to have such a man conducting her wedding ceremony.

He cleared his throat and raised his bible in front of him, eyes shifting to the crowd. "I am happy you all made it out to our Alex's wedding. Now, take a seat and mind your manners and we'll get these two ladies hitched."

A yell of excitement sounded from the pews and Pastor Bruce raised an eyebrow, eyes on the pages in front of him. "I said mind your manners and that means hollerin', William Ansel."

A round of chuckles went through the church and Mary laughed along with them. It felt good to be a part of something so light-hearted and shared. Like a good cup of tea with friends. Mary calmed beside her wife-to-be as the Pastor began their ceremony.

The ceremony was short, sweet, and to the point. Mary was thankful at that, especially knowing her mother was nearby, and in no time at all it was time to exchange their rings and 'I do's.'

Mary uttered hers in a rush. Alex in a measured voice.

The rings were slipped on fingers and then Mary thought she would swoon as Alex drew her close and tilted her head back. The first brush of lips was gentle and seeking, chaste as anything. But Mary nearly did swoon when Alex deepened the kiss, pulling her tight to her. The kiss was short and ended after a moment but...*but*...

There was a spark of passion in her touch. Something needy and hungry that left Mary gasping as they parted. Mary blinked up at her new wife and swallowed hard.

"That was some kiss," she whispered, as she swayed on her feet.

Alex leaned in, a gentle puff of breath tickling Mary's cheeks when the other woman chuckled, and she dropped another to her lips. "Yes, yes, it was, Minnie."

Mary scarcely had time to collect her thoughts before Pastor Bruce was stepping forward and raising their joined hands high in the air. "Let's welcome Missus and Missus Pierce!"

The cheers were deafening but no more so than the staccato beat of Mary's heart.

CHAPTER 9

*M*ary sipped at her punch and glanced around the town square. The space was alive and bright with energy. If she had thought she had seen the town square at its finest for the town fair, she had been mistaken. That event had been a truly memorable night yet paled in comparison to the joyous occasion unfolding in front of her.

And it was all for her wedding.

Or rather Alex's wedding.

She was under no illusion the happy reception was done on her account. Yes, she had married Alex and was involved by proxy, but this was done by the town for Alex. They knew Alex, loved her, wished her to be happy and content. Mary felt her chest tighten as her eyes lighted on her new wife. The other woman cut a fine form in her suit, the setting sun casting a halo of warmth around her handsome face as she laughed, head tossed back, eyes closed, full lips parted.

She dropped her eyes and took another quick swallow.

It would not do to stare at her new wife like a besotted girl. Alex had married her out of kindness, the day unfolding into one of unexpected freedom---pinning lustful and longing desires on Alex was unfair. She wished for her own bit of happiness but would not force it on Alex to uphold.

Mary blew out a breath, her hand going to rest on her stomach. She would find her own happiness in their arrangement. To want more was greedy of her, especially when her life was new and her own. She was free to create a happy home for her baby and herself, even if the road to such a life lay unformed in front of her.

"Mary?"

Her reverie was broken by a familiar voice she couldn't quite place, but she knew it was not her mother and for that she turned towards the voice with a smile.

"Yes--oh, Violet!" Mary nearly dropped her glass of punch in her rush to close the space between them. She came to an ungraceful stop in front of the dark-haired woman and cleared her throat. "I, well, hello! How are you?"

Violet gave her a tentative smile. "I'm well. I'm happy to see you again...I never was able to thank you for what you did for me."

Mary's mouth dropped open. "What? No, I never--"

Violet held out a hand silencing her. "You did do something for us. Please do not say you didn't. If you hadn't intervened that day I saw you and Julian picnicking, well, I--" she paused and dropped her eyes with a little shake of her head, "I never would have considered him, or my feelings, if you had not, ah, put things in such a blunt manner."

Mary chuckled, fingers twirling the punch glass in her hands. "Blunt is quite an apt way to describe my handling of it, but I could not watch you both pine for the other so without speaking up, especially when I played a part in, well, keeping you both apart." She frowned and bit her lip. "I am truly sorry for that, Violet." When the other woman made to speak Mary took a quick step towards her until they were close and continued. If she did not speak her piece now, she feared she might lose her nerve, and a wedding reception seemed as proper as any setting for such an apology.

"I should not have said what I said or allowed my mother to do as she pleased. I should have stopped her that day in the boarding house, and most certainly in the mercantile when she sought to tarnish your reputation. It is a time in my life that I am most ashamed of. I am sorry, Violet. Truly. I do not expect you to forgive me, but I mean to make Gold Sky my home and I hope that you will be able to give me a chance to prove my character to you." Mary gave the other woman a watery smile and found that she could not breathe. In the background she heard laughter, the strum of a guitar and the telltale sound of feet on the makeshift dance floor merry makers were enjoying. Her eyes stayed on Violet. She didn't expect for her to accept her apology, but Mary hoped she would at least be able to begin to make amends to her on this day.

Violet reached out and grasped her hand. "I forgive you."

Mary blinked in surprise. "You do? Just like that?"

"Just like that." Violet squeezed her hand. "It doesn't do well to hold grudges and Julian and I, well, we are leaving Gold Sky soon. It wouldn't do for me to leave with a heavy heart when you expressed yourself so clearly to me then."

"But I was horrible to you."

"We all do things we aren't proud of...and your mother is not a woman I can see allowing for difference of opinion."

"That is true, but I should have--"

"It's all right, Mary. Honestly. I am happy to be here with you and even more glad to know your heart." Violet smiled brightly at her and continued on, "Alex has chosen you as a bride and that has to count for something. You are now a part of Gold Sky. We have a way of taking care of our own. That includes forgiving them when apologies are made."

Mary moved then, throwing her arms around the other woman. Punch sloshed over her cup and onto the ground, but she scarcely paid it much mind in her scramble to embrace Violet.

"Thank you, Violet. Oh, thank you." Mary squeezed her tightly, the feeling of warm happiness Violet's words had given her growing and bubbling up until it was practically spilling over. Violet squeezed her back and when the women parted, they were both smiling at each other.

"When are you leaving town?" Mary asked. "I would like to--"

"Mary Sophia James! What is the meaning of this?"

Mary went stiff. It was her mother, and she sounded none too pleased.

Both women turned to look over their shoulders to take in the sight of Sarah James striding towards them. The crowd of townsfolk parted in front of her like the Red Sea before Moses, and Sarah James was a vengeful Pharaoh.

"Oh no," Mary whispered. "She's here."

"Did she not know you were marrying?" Violet asked.

"She knew, but not in this manner and not now...nor did she know to whom."

"Oh no, oh dear." Violet whispered.

"Oh no is right," Mary moaned. She forced herself to stand tall. She was a married woman, the entire town had seen and even if her mother was unhappy with it, or her, she was no longer beholden to her mother's whims.

"What is going on here?" Her mother jabbed a finger at Mary as she came to a stop in front of her daughter.

"My wedding reception, mother."

"Who did you--what?" Sarah James's eyes went wide at Mary's response. "What do you mean a wedding reception? Why are you in your dress?" She gestured at the plain white dress Mary wore and came forward to snatch her daughter's wrist. "You are meant to wear that to marry Mister Pierce, not parade about with riffraff." Her eyes cut to Violet as she spoke, and Mary felt a surge of anger overtake her. All of the cheer and good feeling her reconciliation with Violet had brokered vanished in an instant, and she snatched her wrist away from her mother.

"Stop it."

"Stop--" Sarah James's mouth dropped open and she

shook her head slowly as if she had been struck. "Stop what?"

"Speaking about Violet like that and-and grabbing me so. Neither are agreeable and I will not have you speaking of one of my guests in such a manner."

"A guest?" Her mother laughed and crossed her arms over her chest. "Your guest is it then? Tell me, what man has you feeling tall enough to raise your voice to your mother?"

"I'm no man."

Mary felt her heartbeat quicken at the familiar sound of her wife's voice. She looked to the side to see her striding close, resplendent in her suit, blonde hair shining like a polished gold halo, her brown eyes stern, and her full lips pressed into a thin line.

"Who are you?" Sarah James asked, her voice rising as she watched Alex come to Mary's side. Her green eyes darted between them and lighted on their hands when Alex moved to take Mary's in hers. Her mother's hands balled into fists and she raised her eyes to her daughter.

"Do not tell me you have done this foolhardy thing."

Mary knew what her mother meant. Her preference for women had always been known without her ever saying the words aloud. Sarah James had always been observant, and she had headed off her daughter at every pass. They both knew what 'foolhardy thing' she referenced. Mary lifted her chin in defiance.

"I have. But my wedding is not foolhardy. It is the one true thing I have done for myself."

Sarah James's eyes shut, and she sucked in a shuddering breath. "Your papa spoiled you rotten," she hissed through clenched teeth. Opening her eyes, she shook her head slowly at her daughter. "First you find yourself compromised, spoiled goods, and now this." She flung a hand out towards the couple and then waved towards the chapel. "Do you know how difficult it will be to remedy this? There is no way Mister Pierce will be foolish enough to take you as a bride now, you stupid girl!"

Mary shook her head and squeezed Alex's hands tighter. "There is no remedying this. I'll not undo it."

"And aside from that, there is no Mister Pierce," Alex interjected with a raised eyebrow.

"What do you know about it? I have the correspondence as proof."

"Yes, you do. From an Alex Pierce, yes."

Sarah James bit her lip and raised an eyebrow at Alex's comment. Mary could see the wheels in her mother's mind spinning wildly. The woman was trying to work out what Alex meant but when she could not, finally gave a stiff nod acknowledgement.

"Yes. And what of it?" she asked.

Alex continued speaking then, "You really ought to not assume things simply by a name. Alex is a fitting name for both a man... and a woman."

Her eyes widened and Sarah James nearly gasped. "You? Alex Pierce, is you?"

Alex nodded. "My full name is Alexandria, but I much prefer Alex. I know you do not approve of the match, but your daughter has married, and she has done it in front of the entire town to boot. There will be no undoing this or sweeping it away. We are married in truth, as wives, with all of Gold Sky as witnesses."

Sarah James staggered back a step at the revelation. "The entire town?" she whispered, hands coming up to rub her temples. She looked at Mary accusingly. "You did this on purpose, you brat. You tricked me! How could you do such a thing to your own mother?"

"I would do it again in a heartbeat," Mary admitted, not shrinking from her mother's accusing eyes. "All my life you have wanted me to be someone I am not, something you wanted to fit into a perfect life. I'm not perfect, mama. I never wanted to be, and now you can't make me do it. I'm a married woman and free of what you want."

For a moment no one said anything. Violet stared at the trio with wide dark eyes. Alex clutched Mary's hand and for her part Mary scarcely found it in her to breathe. Then Sarah James did what she did best. She recovered her sense of decorum and pride as she saw fit.

Mary watched with bated breath as the familiar icy facade her mother preferred slipped into place, the fire went out of her just like that and suddenly it was as if they had never known each other. They were no longer mother and daughter, but two strangers gazing upon one another though Mary's did so with longing and hurt while her mother looked upon her dispassionately.

"You've made your bed then. Make the most of it, as I will not take you back." She then turned on her heel and just as quickly as she arrived, took her leave. Back straight and steps purposeful, Sarah James cut through the crowd. Mary watched her mother's figure until she could no longer distinguish her form from the partygoers. She bit her lip and sagged against Alex with a shake of her head.

"That was dreadful," Violet whispered. "Are you all right?" She asked Mary gently.

Mary was quiet for a moment and then nodded. "Yes, yes, I am. Thank you for asking, Violet." It was painful knowing her mother had left her then, but it was also freeing. Mary had never been under any illusion that her mother would love her as she was, and now with the lines and ties being neatly drawn and cut as they were, Mary was finally able to breathe without the feeling of impending loss looming over her.

"You've got me," Alex told her, drawing her close into an embrace. "I'll never leave you, Minnie. We are family now. You, me, and the little one on the way."

Family.

The one word was enough to make Mary ache and she drank up the steady feel of Alex's arms beneath her hands. They were married, there was no undoing it, the entire town knew of their vows, and even if they were arranged it was quite enough for Mary. Tomorrow she would begin to mourn the loss. But tonight? She smiled up at her wife and felt her heart speed up at the flash of teeth Alex sent her way.

Why, tonight she would celebrate her marriage and her future.

CHAPTER 10

The wagon ride to Alex's, no... *their* new home, Mary reminded herself, was pleasant enough. They were only ten minutes outside of town and she was happy to know she could make the walk if she so chose. She had never driven a wagon and wasn't sure she could manage it, though when she expressed her fears to Alex the other woman had chuckled and told her they would 'learn it together then.'

Together. Mary loved the thought of them doing anything together.

They entered the home, a respectably built cabin, single story with a small porch and a cheery yellow door. She liked that door. Mary also liked the simple but comforting feeling of the cabin. There were handwoven rugs covering the wooden floor and curtains to match the door hanging in the windows. She glanced about the entryway and saw there was not one but two overstuffed settees, a fireplace and a small bookcase full of books. Beyond that she saw what looked to be a combined kitchen and dining room. She paused, looking off to the right where there was a hallway, she took a curious step towards it before Alex spoke from behind her where she was bolting the door.

"The bedrooms and washroom are down that way," she said with a nod of her head. "I can give you a tour now if you like. It's a simple home but we have plenty of room to grow and build as we see fit. It's too dark to show you the barn or the paddock really, but we can walk the land first thing in the morning if you like."

Mary nodded but then paused. "You would allow me a say in how you build?" she asked.

"Of course. This home is yours as much as mine, I mean, for as long as you see fit to be married to me that is. It's all your choice, Mary." Alex gave her a smile and reached out catching her hand. "I'll show you to your bedroom."

Mary nodded and followed along, but she was turning over the words Alex had spoken. 'All her choice.' What precisely did the other woman mean by that? This was of course a favor to her and her unborn child but to hear Alex speak of it...well, Mary had questions. Questions that she hardly knew how to ask on their wedding night.

"It'll have everything you need for now but if there's anything you need write it down and we can order it this week." Alex opened the door to reveal a well-appointed and neat bedroom. There was a canopy bed, a thick woven rug covering the wooden floor, a small plain bedside table holding a basin and pitcher, a chest of drawers, and a writing desk.

Mary walked into the room; arms wrapped around

herself. It was more than enough; it was all perfect. And it was hers. "I love it," she whispered. "Thank you but…" her voice trailed off, lips turning down in a frown as she looked over her shoulder to Alex.

"But what?" Alex asked from her spot by the door. She was leaning against the door frame, a hand on her hip, the other resting on the frame above her head. It was a fine picture and Mary pressed her lips together to stop herself from uttering something foolish. What it might be she couldn't be sure but she had an inkling it would have something to do with her new wife's current enticing pose.

She looked away and licked her lips. "Are you staying somewhere else?" she asked when they came to a stop in front of a door. She paused, daring to look in Alex's direction. "I mean to ask where you'll be sleeping."

Alex's brows knit together, and Mary nearly groaned at her clumsy enquiry. A more refined and skilled lady would have found a subtle turn to ask her question, not stumbled towards it as she had.

Mary cleared her throat and tried again. "What I mean to ask is, ah, is this all for me?" She gestured towards the bed and desk. "It's all too much if it is"

"No."

Mary's heart leaped into her throat at Alex's answer.

"No?" she whispered starting forward, the beginnings of a smile pulling at her lips. If her new wife meant to stay with her, then perhaps there was room enough for her to test the boundaries of their new arrangement. An arrangement that would not have to remain as such, one that could with care and a guidance blossom into more.

Into a relationship.

Alex gave a slight nod of her head and pushed away from the doorway. "No," she said, "my room is just down the hall. You'll holler if you need anything?"

Mary jerked to a stop. Alex's clarification worked as surely as a bucket of cold water to cut through the haze of infatuation she'd been practically swimming in.

"Down the hall. Right, of course." A nervous laugh escaped Mary and she wrapped her arms around herself with a tight smile. "That makes all the sense in the world. I cannot thank you enough for what you did for me. It means everything to me, Alex."

"Of course, it would have been remiss of me to leave a lady such as yourself in such a predicament." Alex raised a hand to her chest and dipped her chin nodding towards Mary. "I was powerless to resist, you know."

"Ah, that makes perfect sense but once more, I must insist that you do not call me a lady. I am no such thing."

Alex scoffed, the sound of it deafening in the quiet bedroom. She crossed the room until she was standing in front of Mary, each and every footstep she took forward causing Mary's heart to pound faster and faster until she was sure Alex must hear the deafening beating of it. Mary watched her wife with wide eyes and the other woman reached out a hand, a fingertip brushing against an errant curl of hair. Mary let out a shuddering breath, eyes riveted to where Alex's finger was gently twisting her hair round and round until she tugged the lock free from the fine hairstyle Alice Hill had painstakingly pulled her hair into for her wedding.

Both women remained silent as Alex raised her free

hand and once more plucked a loose curl to work free from the rest. Alex took another step forward, the length of Mary's skirts pushing up against her legs as she did so. Alex's hand lifted and she buried her fingers into Mary's hair, tugging gently. The full weight of Alex's hand caused her eyes to drift closed, a content sigh slipping from her lips.

"You are as much of a lady as I have ever hoped to know, Minnie."

"Then I fear you have a misunderstanding of what a lady is, but I will not fight you." She opened her eyes and smiled at Alex. "That is, if I am *your* lady." Her jaw snapped shut with an audible click and Mary moved, her feet carrying her away from the blonde. "I mean--ah, I am your wife, so it is, well, I mean if I am a lady then--"

"Then you are mine," Alex finished for her.

"Yes, yours," Mary replied, the words falling from her mouth far too quickly for her to have a prayer of stopping them. Alex held her gaze then, brown eyes burning into her and Mary wished she were braver. If she were then she might have crossed the room and thrown her arms around her new wife, she might have pressed her body close to hers, slanted her mouth to the other woman and taken what she wanted. As it was, Mary was not nearly as brave as she hoped and stayed where she was.

"I like the sound of that," Alex told her. She paused, and for a moment Mary felt the wild hope that she might be the one to come forward flutter wildly in her chest. Though it went still when Alex moved away, her path taking her back, towards the door and most likely her room. That damnable place that was just down the hall and far from where Mary wished Alex to be.

"Goodnight, Minnie."

"Goodnight, Alex."

CHAPTER 11

Farm work was not for the faint of heart. There was nothing gentle about the hours kept on a farm, nor the work to be put in to collecting eggs, milking cows, putting down new hay in stalls, or lifting bags of feed. Mary looked up from the bucket into which she was currently doing her best to coax a respectable portion of milk, to catch a glimpse of her wife exiting the barn, a bag of feed slung over one shoulder.

After an earlier rise than Mary was accustomed to, the pair had shared a quick meal of oats and coffee, with tea for Mary as the smell of coffee had made her stomach turn. From there they had dressed quickly for the cool weather and Mary had been given a tour of the homestead and all of its inhabitants. She was delighted to learn that they were in possession of three dairy cows, five goats, six horses, and a goodly number of hogs and one sweet tempered barnyard cat. Not to mention all of the cattle. There were also the numerous laying hens Alex was now tending to.

Alex had done the lion's share of the labor intensive work that morning but Mary was doing her bit, or at least attempting her best efforts which so far consisted of gathering the morning eggs, helping lay down hay---though Alex hardly let her finish a stall before shooing her out to rest, feeding the barnyard cat, and of course, learning how to milk a cow. Or at least, in theory. It turned out Mary was not a natural when it came to cows, but what she lacked in natural talent she made up for in determination. She gave a quick nod and set upon the cow's udders once more but she had scarcely been at it for a minute or two when the poor creature she had been working on let out a less than pleased sound.

"I'm sorry, this is difficult for me as well," Mary muttered trying to give the cow an awkward pet. Did one pet cows? She frowned and shook her head giving the animal another pet. "I'm sorry, I'm not good at this am I?" she asked, reaching again for the udders with a sigh. "But I promise that if you help me, I will finish quickly, and all I'm asking for is half a pail of milk, which is really hardly anything. Alex tells me you will feel so much better once I'm done."

Mary continued on talking to the animal, head bent low, hands working into a semblance of the rhythm she had observed Alex execute with ease. How was it that she was so damnably bad at this? It should be that difficult, and yet, here she was trying to strike a bargain with a cow as the sun rose.

"What if I bring you two sugar lumps? Cows like those don't they? An apple? Surely you like apples, it would be a lot tastier than the cud you've been eating. I swear it and-

-" she stopped speaking when a spurt of milk hit the side of her pail. She leaned forward to peer into the bucket to see that she had indeed managed to get milk, however slight, from the cow.

"That's lovely!" Mary praised before she tentatively resumed her ministrations. She nearly wept when the cow continued to yield milk for her. "Oh, thank god, I thought I was going to have nothing to show for the morning. You lovely beast, you!"

"She's prone to taking bribes, it seems."

Mary smiled at Alex's voice and continued working, though this time there was a slight lift of her head and she did her best to showcase her posture as difficult as it may be while milking a cow.

"Is she now?" she asked.

"Oh, yes, and she adores apples." Alex came to stand beside the cow and gave its head a stroke. "Isn't that right, Andromeda?"

"That's quite the name for a cow as humble as this."

Alex chuckled and leaned her head against the cow's forehead giving it's ears a scratch. The gesture reminded Mary of what one might do with a loveable dog or pet and she stopped milking to lean back to watch her wife. There was affection in her actions, not at all like what she thought a rancher would show their livestock, and it was a lovely sight to see.

"Who said she's humble?" Alex looked away from the cow to Mary a jerk of her chin towards the stalls where the other cows were. "Why her sisters Medusa and Cassiopeia show that she comes from quite the storied background."

"That's quite an affluent group to socialize within," Mary said and smiled, leaning forward once more to continue her task. "Perhaps I judged too quickly."

"I would say that you did, but it is an understandable mistake."

"Oh, is it?"

Alex lowered her voice and leaned closer to where Mary sat. "Oh, yes, the thing is that Andromeda is quite shy and does not disclose such facts about herself to new acquaintances. However," she shrugged and smiled as she spoke, "for an apple she will perform or divulge a goodly number of secrets."

Mary laughed and leaned back on her stool. Her task was complete, and the bucket was well over half full with milk. She had done well, and she smiled broadly up at Alex. "I see that I settled too easily if such things can be bought with a single apple.'

"It's true. You did. But it is a common mistake. Now that you know, you may strike a better bargain, hmm?" She inclined her head and Mary felt her breath catch, whatever blithe reply she was about to make dying on her lips the moment the rising sun lit upon Alex's hair. The honeyed golden hues of it were brightened and made warm, coming to life like firelight in the early morning and she blinked in surprise.

Who would have known that seeing her wife in such a domestic scene, one that was so utterly and completely common would render her speechless?

"Are you well?" Alex raised an eyebrow and lifted a hand, a beautifully formed hand to push back the hair that had fallen into her face.

"I--sorry?" Mary blinked and remembered to breathe. She steadied herself with a hand on Andromeda's side and focused back on Alex to see that her wife was staring at her.

"You look as if you might faint." Alex squatted down beside her and placed a hand to her cheek. "Is it the baby? Do you need to lay down for a spell?"

"I-well, no, no. I'm fine." Mary swallowed thickly and pushed back, rising from the stool though every part of her body screeched at her to stay where she was, her body so close to Alex's, the other woman's thighs brushing her skirts, concerned hands on her face as they were. But this was not a marriage of love or even lust. It was one born of necessity and kindness. She would not take more than was offered to her, she would not, she would not, she would not.

And with a choked sigh Mary rose from her seat and gave her wife a bright smile. She raised the pail and motioned towards the house. "I'll just see this in and then come back to deal with Andromeda and--"

"No, no," Alex waved a hand and stood. "There's no need to fuss. I'll handle her. You put that away and stay indoors for a bit. I'll come in and we can see to the list of things you might need to purchase."

Mary stopped in surprise. "Purchase?"

"Yes, for the house. I reckon you'll be inclined to set it up in a way that agrees with you." Alex gestured at the barn and gave her a rueful smile. "I'm more inclined to the outdoors and the house may be lacking in comforts I hadn't thought of."

Mary bobbed her head and gave a quick murmur of thanks before she turned and hurried towards the house. It was only when she entered the home that she realized she hadn't the slightest clue what to do with a pail full of milk.

～

"WHAT DO YOU MEAN 'MY ACCOUNTS?'" Mary asked, looking down at the neat notebook of papers Alex had slid across the table to her moments before.

"Exactly what I said, Minnie. Your accounts. Inside you'll find all the information you need to access your account at the bank, and there's paper enough in there to keep an accurate balance. I'll make deposits regularly and you are free to add as you wish to it. I have already sent word to the mercantile, grocer, bookstore and dress shop that you will be in today to begin your own lines of credit."

"My own...lines of credit?" Mary felt foolish parroting every word Alex spoke to her, but it was almost too much to believe and she swallowed thickly at the news. Her mother had never so much as given Mary anything more than pocket money and only enough to buy a meal here or there. Her father had ensured Mary was set up with accounts but those had all been closed and lost to her with his passing. Her fingers touched the coarse material of the bank book and she could scarcely breathe as she flipped it open to find her name typed in neat script.

Minnie Pierce.

Her eyes filled with tears. It was a lovely sight, one that touched her far deeper than she realized. "You had them put my name as Minnie," she said simply.

"I did," Alex said and then she cleared her throat and gave her wife a pained look. "Ought I not to have? I mean….well, it's just that I've thought of you as nothing else but Minnie," she hurried on to add when Mary gave a slight sniffle, "but we can have it changed first thing to Mary. It'll be an easy fix, you'll see." Alex pulled a hand-kerchief out and held it out to Mary with a grimace. "Oh, I've made a right mess of this haven't I? I'm sorry, Min-- Mary, please don't cry. I'm an idiot and---"

Mary reached out, catching her wife's hand and gave a quick shake of her head. "No, don't say it like that."

"Say it like what?"

"*Mary*," she said, voice scarcely above a whisper and she sniffled past her tears as she spoke. "Call me Minnie. Please, Alex. I--that's what I would have you call me."

"Then why are you crying so?"

"These are happy tears." Mary laughed when Alex gave her an unconvinced look. "I swear it."

"Do you promise?" Alex leaned across the table and pointed a finger at her wife with a solemn look. "Swear it now, or I'll have them change it."

Mary gave a shaky laugh. "I swear it, Alex. I do. I love it. She raised the bank book. "I love this, and I-I would have you call me nothing else than Minnie. I swear it."

Alex looked at her for a moment longer before she nodded and relaxed. "I'm awful when you take to crying. You'll see. I've never been any good at it."

"It's only tears."

Alex snorted. "To you perhaps, but I have no clue how to help or stop them. Tears are-are…"

"What are they?"

"Frightening is what they are." Alex crossed her arms over her chest and shook her head. "You'll never know the fear they strike into the hearts of good spouses across the world." She clasped a hand to her chest in emphasis making Mary giggle.

"You're quite dramatic Alex."

"Right you are." Alex winked at her. "Makes life a bit more tolerable, don't you think?" She reached out and took Minnie's hand as she stood from her chair and pressed a slight kiss to her knuckles. "I'll be outside seeing to the horses. Get your things together for the journey into town, hmm?"

"Ah, yes," Mary managed to get out. "I'll be there shortly," she said. Alex gave a wave of her hand and continued on, her footfalls slowly fading and then going silent as she left the house. Once the door shut behind her Mary sagged back against her chair and let out the ragged sigh she hadn't been aware she was holding in.

"Oh, dear," she whispered, hands going to her face. She held up the hand Alex had kissed in front of her, the gesture had been so casually done and without thought that Mary found it all the more precious and significant. It was as if they had been together for far longer than their scant day of marriage, their handful of acquaintances, as if the other woman had never been without her. That kisses should pass so freely and easily between them was a thing that made Mary's heart flutter and she shifted, leaning forward onto the table holding the hand up in front of her with wide eyes.

Perhaps her marriage was not purely of kindness after all.

CHAPTER 12

"You mean that I am free to choose whatever I like?" Mary asked. She was currently standing in front of the mercantile with a hastily scribbled list she had put together on their ride into town. She bit her pencil and looked at her wife curiously when Alex rocked back on her heels and gave her a nod.

"Yes, whatever you like. Pick it out and we'll have it packed up. The shop will settle the bill with me at the end of the month. I'll be just up the way talking with Stark about a set of rockers I've had on my mind to get. Now is just as good a time as any." Alex made to move away, and Mary found herself unable to stagger towards her wife with an outstretched hand.

"And you...won't need to look it over?" she asked.

"No," Alex answered, and then paused looking back at Mary, "is there a reason I would need to Minnie?"

Mary stopped and considered her words. In her life she had been trusted with precious little. Her mother had always been at the forefront of all decisions, even down to the color of dresses Mary wore, or how she curled her hair. Her father had allowed her some freedom, but it had always been the root of an argument between her parents and led to a sour dinner with all three in tense silence. Mary had learned from a young age to want for little and to ask for less.

"Well, no, I suppose you would not need to but I--" Mary's voice trailed off when she saw a flash of red and saw it was nothing less than her mother's hair. Sarah James was beautifully done up in the dress Mary had last seen her fitted in.

Her wedding dress.

In her hand was a bouquet of white roses and on her arm was a dapper dressed Mister Rutherford. It seemed the elder James could not be outdone by her daughter's impromptu wedding and so had secured one of her own after all.

Mary paused when her mother looked her way and she saw the familiar icy stare aimed at her. Sarah James tossed her head, her red curls cascading over her shoulder as she walked, head high and body elegantly poised as ever, there was not a care on her mother's face--save for her attention to Mister Rutherford. Her mother always did have an uncanny ability to focus on those she deemed useful and Mary saw now that it was aimed at her new husband.

"Should I stay by your side?" Alex murmured and took a step closer to her. They were nearly shoulder-to-shoulder now, fingers almost brushing, arms grazing the other, and Mary did not miss how her wife drew herself up to her full height when she noticed the newly married couple crossing the avenue and making their way towards them.

"I-well, I don't rightly know," Mary confessed when she realized she was unable to determine how her mother might act in the moment. "I've never been one to know what my mother might do."

"I'll stay put then."

Mary dipped her chin in acknowledgement and felt strengthened by the barest brush of Alex's fingers against the back of her knuckles. She cautioned a look up at her wife then and felt the same overwhelming sense of awe at her beauty. It was raw and pure, unfiltered and so genuine in its simple way of being. Alex didn't try to conform or school her features into a palatable way, not as Mary had been taught. The woman *simply was*, and Mary could not be more grateful for it.

"I see we are not the only newlyweds in town." Mister Rutherford greeted them with a tip of his hat and smiled warmly at Mary. "It's a shame I missed such a fine event, Mary. I hear it was a truly memorable night."

"It was...dramatic, or so I have read in the morning paper." Her mother sniffed and looked at her daughter as if she scarcely knew her, and Mary knew the prior evening's words had not been hastily exchanged. This wasn't her mother. It wasn't even Sarah James. It was Missus Rutherford and there wasn't a soul on the avenue that didn't know it.

"Yes, it was a joyous time enjoyed by all." Alex reached for her then, lacing their fingers together. "I am pleased to see that you have been able to take part in your own bit of happiness as well," she said, giving the couple a smile that could have fooled Mary as genuine, except that in their small time together she had noticed quite a lot about her wife and it all told her the smile she aimed at the newly christened Mister and Missus Rutherford was anything but amicable.

It was guarded and pointed. There would be no lingering. Not if the couple was smart.

Mary watched as Mister Rutherford took note. His eyes drifting from Alex to his new wife and then finally to Mary. He watched her for a moment, and she managed a quick "Hello," with a nod of her head to her mother. She was not keen on sparring with the newly minted Sarah Rutherford.

"Ah, well, we were just here to see to a few things," Mister Rutherford told them, pointing towards the mercantile. "I expect you are as well."

"We are. Minnie is in need of a few items and there's no time like the present."

Mary was glad she was facing away from her mother, her hand in Alex's who was leading her up the stairs, and away from the couple at their back. If she had been facing forward she might have caught sight of her mother's face when the strangled sound at their back came out of her mouth, she might have also seen the curious shade of red her mother's face became as she spluttered as well.

As it was, she missed both occurrences. Though the sounds her mother was making were anything but lady-like. A smile touched her lips at the near snorting and strangled scoff coming from her mother.

"Are you well, my dear?" Mister Rutherford asked, and Mary had to fight back the laugh bubbling in her chest.

The man would be caught unawares by his new wife's behavior, but that, like everything associated with Mary's mother, was none of her daughter's concern any longer.

Mary turned towards Alex and smiled at the sight of her strong wife. The blonde was still holding her hand, the sure and steady feel of her palm against Mary's made her feel as if all would be well. Alex was ahead of her, leading her towards the tidy aisles of the mercantile. There were rows of sundries and dry goods, along with a good section of material, fine shoes and stockings, and even delicacies such as scented French soap and expensive perfumes Mary recalled from her days of primping.

She paused in front of a small display of glass bottles. She reached out tentatively when one of the bottles caught her eye but stopped short of touching it. She did not recognize the label, nor the name, *Rococo*, but the unmistakable name of Guerlain assured her of its quality. The bottle was small and lovely with its gold and blue label, the glass stopper at the top beckoned to her, begging for her to pull it free and indulge her senses. It had been quite some time since Mary had smelled of anything other than the soap she used to wash, and even then, the light floral of the bars was long gone by the afternoon hours.

Mary bit her lip, eyes fastened on the bottle and her fingers twitched as she nearly reached for it. To purchase the bottle would be nothing but a luxury, a bit of frivolity and wholly unneeded. If she wanted to prove her worth and mettle to her new wife, it was an item she should surely pass up. She bit back a sigh and nodded to herself at the decision to walk away from the perfume. She did not need it, nor would she use her new fiscal trust from Alex on such an unnecessary item. She was here to outfit a home, not satisfy her baser need for indulgence, Mary moved to step away and stopped short when she realized Alex had moved closer. Their still clasped hands were pressed close to Alex's side and she leaned in to see what had caught Mary's attention.

"Do you, ah," Alex cleared her throat and nodded at the perfume display, "are any of these to your liking?"

"Oh yes! These are of the finest quality and I used to wear many of them when I was home in Texas," Mary blurted out and then winced at the quickness of her answer. "I mean to say that they are...interesting."

"Interesting hmm?" Alex looked up at her briefly before her brown eyes were once more on the glass bottles.

"Yes, interesting. But not needed," Mary replied firmly and tugged on her wife's hand. "Should we continue with our shopping--"

"Which one would you like?"

Mary's eyes widened at Alex's question. "What do you mean?"

"I mean, which one of these would you like to own." Alex jerked her chin towards the bottles. "You looked as if you might touch this one here, the one with the blue and gold label?"

"Ah, yes, that one is new," Mary admitted. "But I don't need it," she added quickly when Alex dropped her hand and reached for the bottle. Mary's fingers twitched, her palm itching to be in contact once more with Alex's. She would give up the entire perfume display a hundred times over if she were only able to have Alex's hand in hers once more.

"Just because you don't need it doesn't mean you don't deserve it," Alex told her. "If you want this then we should--"

"Already getting your little fill of baubles, hmm? Smart girl. I raised you right then." The words were uttered in passing by Mary's mother and Mary felt the blood drain from her face when Alex stopped speaking. The blonde turned, watching Sarah, ahem, Rutherford, sashay by. The other woman was making quite the show of browsing the aisles, but Mary knew her mother better. There was no way she wasn't tracking her and Alex's conversation, cataloguing their interactions, what they were doing.

Why she saw fit to do it, Mary couldn't say but she hated it. She stepped closer to Alex and placed a hand on her arm. "Please, can we put it back and forget about it."

Alex gave a quick shake of her head. "She's trying to control you," she said, looking at Mary with a stern frown on her face, full lips pressed into a thin line, "to control us by planting ugly seeds like that. I'm getting this for you, and that's that."

"Bu--"

"No buts, Minnie. You wanted it and it's my right to spoil my new bride if I so choose, now isn't it?" Alex raised a hand and tilted Mary's face up to hers with the tip of her forefinger. The breath caught in her chest, as it often did when Alex's attention was focused on her and Mary felt a slight tremble run through her body. It was the slightest thing, that gentle touch, nothing more than a press of finger to chin but it did wonders for Mary. She smiled up at her wife for lack of a better or smarter thing to do.

The two women stood as they were, bodies close but not touching, faces angled towards the other, Mary almost leaned into her. So close were they she could feel the warmth of Alex's body through her dress. She licked her lips and Alex's brown eyes tracked the movement. Alex's finger slid up from her chin, the light sensation of it sent a shot of adrenaline through her body. Mary knew her eyes were wide, body held tight as a bowstring, when Alex's finger stopped its quest at her bottom lip. She leaned close to Mary, flattening her finger, the pressure causing lightning to move straight down her legs.

"Allow me to buy it," Alex said once she was close enough to whisper. Mary's eyes drifted closed and the world around her ceased to exist. It mattered not that she was in the mercantile, or that her mother was nearby looking for any sign of weakness she might think to use against her. Against them.

"You'll let me do that won't you?" Alex's breath puffed warm against her skin, the barest brush of her lips grazing Mary's cheek.

Mary opened her eyes to see Alex looking down at her intently. There was a yearning there she felt she understood and was helpless to ignore.

"I suppose so," Mary murmured after a moment. She might have said more and even thought to lean into her urge to move closer, to take Alex's mouth for her own, but just then the shopkeeper made to wait on them. Alex withdrew from her and Mary nearly pouted at the loss of her wife's touch as she made to stand behind her.

"Alex, how are you?" He greeted them with a warm smile. "Your wedding was lovely. I've not had the pleasure of meeting the new missus."

"Pleased to meet you. I am Mary Ja-" she stopped, catching herself as she fumbled with her new surname, "Pierce. Mary Pierce."

Mary was thankful her social training took over then and she managed to compose herself enough to make her introductions properly. Behind her Alex merely grunted and placed the bottle of perfume on the counter with a thud.

"We will take this. Add it to our order please. And whatever Minnie likes."

The shopkeeper's eyebrows drew up at the name. "Minnie?"

"Oh, ah, she means me," Mary offered with a quick smile. "It's a nickname," she explained.

He nodded, picking up the bottle of perfume. "Minnie it is then. It suits you perfectly."

Mary beamed at the man, unable to keep the smile off her face at his words. "Thank you."

"Anytime, Mrs. Pierce. Please let me know if I can assist you with anything. I'll have this at the front waiting for you."

Mary turned towards Alex and grinned at her. Alex was frowning in the direction of the shopkeeper and she sighed, stepping closer to her. "Why the sour look?"

Alex's eyes flicked towards her and almost instantly the woman went soft. She sighed and shook her head, blonde hair gleaming in the morning light that shone brightly through the mercantile windows.

"Small annoyances really," she said, lifting one shoulder in a shrug, "but it was all for the best I suppose."

"Oh?" Mary asked, walking past her to look at a collection of fine lace curtains. They were light and airy, just the thing to let in a good bit of sunlight while softening the hard edges of the utilitarian homestead life.

"Mmm, all for the best," Alex said again, and this time she was smiling at her. "Do you want those as well?" she gestured towards the curtains in Mary's hands.

"These?" Mary looked down at the material she had been considering and bit her lip. They would be lovely in the kitchen. She ran her fingers over the lace of it and tilted her head to the side considering the fine stitches. A haughty laugh sounded a few feet away and though Mary did not lift her head she knew it was her mother, and what was more, she knew it was done for effect.

Her mother did nothing without cause. Even now she was most likely keeping an eye on Mary, gauging her reaction and how she interacted with Alex, but Mary found she no longer had the patience to care what her mother thought.

She lifted her head, but she did not look towards her mother's telltale red hair, instead her eyes were on Alex, and Alex alone, the lace curtains in hand.

"I do. I want them very much."

Her life had been spent for far too long worried over her mother's wants and motivations---now Mary's only motivation was how to fulfill her dreams, and those were living a good life in Gold Sky. And she was coming to see that life, thankfully, included a wife like Alex Pierce.

A CRACK of lightning sounded overhead, the bright flash of it illuminated the sitting room and Mary looked away from her book with a frown of concern. She had known that it would rain but this...this was an impending storm. The sound of rain falling fast and hard on the roof drew her attention to the ceiling and she swallowed hard at the sudden roar that filled her ears.

This was no storm. This was a raging tempest in every sense of the word, and she turned to look over her shoulder in the direction of the back door. She rose from her chair and made her way towards the kitchen. Alex was out in the downpour; she had left hours before dead set on mending a line of fence for fear that the turning weather would drive their cattle to scatter.

"It'll only take an hour or so at most. I'll be home long before the rain arrives."

Mary's hands twisted in her skirts at the memory of Alex's words. It was achingly similar to her father's reassurances, and the fright she felt bubbling up in her chest was to be expected. Another gale of rain let loose on the home and the windows rattled in their frames. A glance at the windows showed little was visible beyond the panes. If Mary was unable to see, then it went without saying that Alex was blind out in the downpour. How was the other woman finding her way back? What if she were lost and--?

"Stop it," Mary chastised herself. "This is not the time to lose your head. Stop it." She squeezed her eyes shut and inhaled deeply. She could do this. She would stay calm and all would be well. When she felt surer of herself she made to start towards the door but stopped short when a sharp pain in her side caused her to falter. She shook her head and put a hand out against the wall with a wince at the ache. Her free hand went to her belly, there was no mistaking that the discomfort she felt must in some way be associated with the baby but how and why?

Mary took in a careful measured breath and focused on staying calm. Now was not the time for her to panic, not when Alex was still missing, and the storm raged on. She must keep a calm head and work to relax. It was then that the downpour was useful, the roar of the rain dulled her senses and she breathed deeply using it to her advantage in this moment. She bowed her head, forehead coming to rest against the wall and breathed in again and again, so focused on her breath was Mary that she missed the opening and resounding slam of the back door. It was only when she felt Alex's hands on her shoulders that she realized her wife had returned.

"Minnie? Are you well? What is it?" Alex's worried voice was a welcome respite from the deafening storm. "What happened?"

"Nothing, nothing, I'm fine. I promise." Mary looked up from the wall to see her wife gazing at her with a worried expression. Her normally warm brown eyes were wide with concern as she looked Mary over. She leaned back, her eyes moving over Mary's face and body as if she were taking stock.

"You do not look well, Minnie."

Mary husked out a laugh and pushed away from the wall. "I am fine. It's you that I feared for."

Alex's eyebrows knit together. "Me?" she asked and once more reached for Mary.

"Yes, you."

"There was nothing to worry over, now come with me."

"I disagree on that matter entirely," Mary told her but she went with Alex all the same.

"And why is that?" Alex asked, guiding her towards the settee.

Mary flung an arm out towards the storm that still raged and glared at Alex. "The storm, of course! How could I not worry?"

Alex waved a hand at her. "Storms like this are normal, Minnie. It's no reason to worry yourself, and especially not when you're with child." She crouched down in front of her and placed her hands on Mary's side. "Can you breathe?"

Mary swatted at her hands. "I--yes, I'm fine." She felt the anxiety she had been harboring that evening bubble once more to the surface and she shook her head in frustration. "I thought I could have lost you," she told Alex, her voice cracking, and it was then the other woman looked up from her ministrations.

"Minnie? What is it?"

"You could have never returned."

"But I did. I have. I am here now."

"But," Mary sucked in a deep breath, her eyes closing, hands balling into fists, "that has--sometimes people do not return."

Alex bit her lip and went still at her wife's words. "Who was it?" she asked, her voice gentle.

Mary blinked at her question. "Who what?" she asked looking down at her wife properly for the first time. Her memories of her father's departure had driven her anxiety to new levels and in her state, she had looked any and everywhere other than her wife. She paused now and placed her hands on Alex's cheeks and looked upon her until she felt the ache in her chest subside.

"Who didn't return?" Alex asked once more. She raised her hands and placed them over Mary's. "It was someone dear to you, I can see that now."

Mary's fingers tensed slightly against Alex's cheeks and she was silent for a moment before she drew in a deep breath and answered her wife. "My father."

"Oh Minnie. Minnie, no." Alex moved then and took her wife in her arms, gathering her close to her and she pressed a kiss to Mary's forehead. "No, darling, I'm so sorry. When you told me that you had lost your father, I did not assume that it was so recent. It was recent wasn't it?"

Mary nodded; her cheek pressed to Alex's shoulder. "Yes, he died at sea, and--and," she faltered then, a sob she hadn't been aware was building shook her body. "He told me that he would return and there was nothing to worry over, but that wasn't true. It wasn't true."

"Minnie."

"You said the same thing before you left and the storm, it came so suddenly, I thought anything could have happened to you." Mary shook her head and drew back to look up at Alex. "I couldn't bear the thought of losing you. I couldn't even think it."

"You'll never lose me, Minnie. Never."

"How can you say that? Anything can happen and--"

"Fear is no way to live, Minnie. There is nothing to fear between us, not when I love you as I do. There isn't a moment that I don't wish to be with you, and I will always return to you. I am yours."

Mary's hands tightened on Alex's soaked jacket. "What did you say?"

Alex raised an eyebrow but repeated herself all the same. "Fear is no--"

"Not that part."

"Then what part would you have me repeat?"

"The part where you say you love me."

CHAPTER 13

"*I* love you."

Three simple words had never changed Mary's world quite so succinctly. They were only words, and words, Mary had learned in the form of broken promises uttered by lovers, or her mother's compulsion for lies, could and did mean very little.

But these words--Alex's words meant everything to Mary.

"I love you," Mary had said in return. They had stared at one another then, the deafening sound of the storm the only sound save for their breathing but even that was now lost to the storm's fury. She wrapped her arms around Alex's shoulders and pulled the other woman to her in a kiss that was neither gentle nor unsure. It was hungry and needy, and as powerful as the tempest raging around them.

"I love you," she said again when they parted. The kiss had left them breathless and staring as if they had never clapped eyes on the other until this moment. And perhaps they never had, not truly. There was nothing between them but the truth now and with it came love and passion, and most of all need.

Alex's lips pulled into a slow smile and she rose to her feet, bringing Mary with her. "Come with me, Minnie." She turned, leading Mary in the direction of the bedroom, though they only made it to the hallway before Mary was once more reaching for Alex. She smoothed her hands over her muscular shoulders and, raising herself up on her tiptoes, slanted her mouth to Alex's in another eager kiss.

Alex moaned, her mouth opening to Mary's questing tongue and she swept the smaller woman up against her. "Minnie. My beautiful Minnie. I love you," She whispered against Mary's lips. "I love you."

A heat swept through Mary's body and she swore there wasn't a part of her that did not crave Alex's strong hands and fingers. She arched her back seeking to be closer and laughed when they bumped awkwardly into the wall and then once more off the doorframe. She supposed it may have been easier to make their way to her bed if they had thought to separate but there wasn't a less appealing action to her than letting go of Alex. Although she did so reluctantly as the other woman insisted on lighting a fire.

"I need to see you," Alex told her once the fireplace was coaxed to life. She crossed the room and dropped to her knees in front of Mary and reached for her foot. She undid the laces of her boots with a patience and focus Mary admired. She, on the other hand, was anything but focused and leaned forward yanking the still dripping coat from Alex's body with a fumbling jerk of her hands. It landed in a sopping mess on the floor and she knew their impassioned journey to her bed would be a nightmare to clean up... but it would also be entirely worth it. She would relish every second they spent cleaning mud and water from their home. Each and every drop of it would remind her of this night and of the fulfillment she found in it.

"May I undress you?" Alex asked. She was still kneeling in front of Mary, and the effect of it was nearly too much for her sensibilities to handle. Her wife cut a very fine image.

"Yes, you may. I insist, actually. Please *do*," she said, the last word lingering and heavy with the yearning Mary felt for the other woman's touch. "I need your hands on me."

"Do you?" Alex asked as she rose to her feet, her hands trailing slowly up Mary's legs, thighs, and then finally her sides.

"Yes, *yes.*"

"And how much do you need my hands on you, my Minnie?"

"If you were to stop touching me I would stop breathing, I would-I would," Mary threw her hands up and shook her head, very nearly stamping her foot as she placed her hands on Alex's and pressed them close to her. "I feel as if I might die if you were to take your hands from me."

Alex's eyes darkened, the rain droplets glistening on her lush lashes as her golden hair glittered in the firelight. The warmth of the fire softened her wife's normally sharp features into something entrancing, intoxicating even, and Mary shook her head in disbelief at the raw beauty in front of her, touching her.

"Then I shall never stop touching you." Alex's fingers flexed. The weight of her touch on Mary's waist made her shiver with anticipation and when her wife carefully turned her to face away, she found she was nearly trembling.

"I'm going to undress you now," Alex told her, the other woman's voice was low and gravely, hoarse in all the very best manner of ways. The tone of it filled Mary's mind with images of early morning fog on a lake, of the way the mountains broke through the mist at the first sunlight, it was base in need—powerful in its existence because it demanded Mary as she craved to be needed, desired.

Mary nodded her permission and stood with shaking hands, back to her wife, her eyes fixed on the fire that was still coming to life. It had come quite a long way in such little time, from the embers and first sparks. Now long flames licked at the fire grate, the wood inside popping and crackling as it continued to grow. Before long it would consume the logs in a blaze Mary was sure could take them, house and all, were it not safely contained in its proper place. She felt much like that fire, slowly coming to life beneath Alex's skilled hands. Until she was capable of taking them both, if it were not that she too, like the fire, were precisely where she belonged.

Alex's fingers worked on the buttons of her dress as surely as if she were not attempting to do so after a hard ride and dripping from the downpour. Mary's mind drifted to what she would be capable of when her fingers weren't in danger of freezing, but that was not now and now...now Mary had Alex, freezing hands and all, at her back and working her dress free. She swallowed, the pulse at the base of her throat jumping when her dress loosened and slid down to her ankles. She stepped forward and out of the dress at the gentle press of Alex's hands at the small of her back. Goose flesh rose on her skin despite the warmth of the room. She was standing in only her under-things and Mary was under no illusion that anything other than the woman behind her was responsible for the pebbling of her skin. Alex stepped in close, hands once more coming to rest lightly on the curves of her sides and the woman inhaled sharply when she surveyed the state of the corset Mary wore.

"Oh Minnie, why have you been hiding this from me?"

"Hiding? Hiding what?" She looked over her shoulder at Alex to see an expression of sorrow and consternation painting her beautiful features.

"This," Alex said, pressing lightly on the corset she wore. She ran a finger up the length of one seam, her touch ginger on the boning that dug painfully into Mary's side. "This is constricting, Minnie. Why are you wearing it so tightly? Can you breathe?"

She bit her lip and looked down at the garment. Alex's fingers were stark against the cream material, the material that was laced as tightly as Mary was able to manage. Morning after morning she had done it under the careful watch and direction of her mother but now...why had she kept doing it?

There was no reason to hide her baby from Alex, no reason to hide the way her body was changing, rounding and softening in the particular way that came with child-bearing. The baby was a gift of life Mary desperately wanted and yet...she continued to dress with the same care and rigidity she displayed under her mother's direction.

"I don't rightly know," she confessed. Mary gave a quick shake of her head and put a hand over her belly with a frown as she turned over Alex's question. Could she breathe? Was it affecting the baby?

"The baby," she said, suddenly rushing to undo the stays of the corset. "What have I been doing? I kept doing it up so tight and there was no need. I don't--why did I keep doing it?" Her words were coming quicker now, voice high and tinny at the realization that she had caused harm to her child out of habit.

When her fingers fumbled Alex shushed her gently. "Let me," she murmured, stepping closer to Minnie, bringing their bodies flush. The feel of Alex's chest and the press of her breasts against her back made Mary still and she simply nodded as the other woman began to undo the tight corset laces.

"Oh, Minnie. *My Minnie*," Alex sighed and tutted as the laces came loose to reveal inch after inch of Mary's abused skin. There were angry red marks on her skin from the boning and corset laces, those tender bruised places were met with Alex's gentle touch. Mary sighed in relief as she was finally allowed the room to breathe freely. When the corset fell away she nearly dissolved into relieved laughter.

"I never want to wear that again," Mary declared, her voice wavered from the sudden rush of air to her lungs, but she was sure of herself. All her life she had wished for freedom and it had been a hard-won thing. Somehow still she had tried to fit herself into a life no longer fit for herself. She would never do that again, and she would not raise her child to do the same.

They would be free to be whomever they wished. To love whomever they wished.

"You never will," Alex agreed. She lowered her head and dropped a kiss onto Mary's shoulders, hands gently caressing the welts left behind by her corset. Her skin tender, Mary winced, but she sighed as the initial sting of Alex's touch dissolved into pleasure. Though her flesh was over sensitized it desperately craved her wife's touch and it was a joy to receive it so freely. Alex laced their fingers together, palm over the back of Mary's hand the heat of it---the very closeness made Mary's insides go molten. There was something erotic in the mundaneness of it. They were holding hands, it should not be affecting her as it was, but as it were, they were closer than they had ever been in that simple touch.

She closed her eyes and leaned her head back against Alex's chest, chin tipped up to the ceiling. Alex's lips grazed her ear, cheek, and then finally her jaw as the other woman kissed her way to the column of Mary's throat. It was there that her breath caught when Alex's mouth brushed her neck. Mary leaned back, her weight supported by Alex as she kissed Mary, lips and tongue peppering the expanse of her flesh, hands cupping her breasts. Mary gasped, the sound transforming into a moan when Alex's fingers teased her nipples. She palmed Mary's flesh, cradling her breast. The touch ignited a fire at Mary's core, and she opened her eyes to see Alex looking down at her as if she were the most wondrous thing she had ever seen.

As if she were the only woman in the world. She lifted a hand to Alex's face and cupped her cheek. The two women stared at one another for a breath before Mary managed to find her voice.

"Take me to bed."

Alex's eyes darkened, awe transforming to lust in an instant and the blonde didn't answer. Not with words anyhow. She merely set herself into motion and swept her wife up into her arms and covered Mary' mouth with her own. The kiss was everything Mary had ever dreamed of, passion and need, made into action. She reached out, hands seeking to get a grip on the rain-soaked material and when it stuck to her wife's skin she nearly growled in frustration. The damnable cotton needed to be done away with and in quick order.

"I'll do it," Alex chuckled, seeing her wife's narrowed eyes.

Mary nodded her hands falling uselessly at her sides. "It must come off."

And off it came as they tumbled onto the bed. Alex rose to her knees, she was lying between Mary's parted legs, thighs pressed thighs as she undid and removed her shirt. She had scarcely tossed it to the side when Mary's hands were once more upon her.

"You're beautiful," Mary told her, looking upon her in earnest. Everywhere she looked, she touched. "So beautiful." Alex leaned forward, a hand going to the back of Mary's head, hands tangling in her hair and holding her up, so the couple were able to kiss while Mary explored the planes and dips of Alex's body. It was a lovely thing to behold, all hard muscle beneath soft skin creating an irresistible territory to explore. Their kiss was slow now, slower than it had been in the sitting room, and slower still than in their hurried rush to enter the bedroom. In her stolen illicit moments with women Mary had always been forced to hurry for fear they would be seen, and their reputations left in ruin. Fumbling hands and teeth on teeth, bruising kisses and whispers to be silent in the empty drawing rooms and powdering rooms of society's upper echelon. She had never been afforded the privilege of exploring a lover as she did now in the comfort and safety of her own home. Their coupling was languid, kisses measured and lingering. Oh, there was softness in this type of passion—it felt real and sustainable. Easy as all things slow did.

Mary found she liked slow.

They parted then and brown met green in a look that could only be seeking. "I aim to give you and our baby a good life." vowed Alex.

"You already have." Mary laughed then and kissed her wife once more. "You've given it everything."

"Then I have yet more to give." Alex shifted back and settled between her thighs, and Mary's hips lifted in eagerness that put a chiding smile on Alex's lips.

She bowed her head forward as if in supplication and began to tease and kiss the flesh beneath her. Mary groaned hands going to the quilts beneath them when Alex's tongue began to circle that delicate bundle of nerves. First gently and then gradually with increasing pressure, her fingers joined in her love play and by the time her wife took her bud into her mouth Mary was fit to faint.

"Please," she begged, lifting her head to look down at Alex. "Please, Alex."

Her wife looked up at her then, blonde hair gleaming as brightly as a halo to her. She could have asked Mary for anything then. She would have agreed to it all if only to summit the wave of ecstasy on which she had been driven higher and higher stil. Oh, what the sight of her wife between her thighs did to her. It ignited her, and her blood went hotter even still when Alex turned her attention back to her, eyes meeting hers even as she continued to suck and lick her. Alex reached up, fingers splaying across the rounded curve of Mary's belly. The gesture was possessive and tender all at once, and Mary only lasted but a few more seconds under her wife's attention. Her back bowed off the bed and she peaked with a shout of release.

"Alex!" Her name was torn from Mary's lips in a ragged sob that left her shaking, hands pressed to her face and breath coming painfully short. Alex slipped from her remaining clothes and joined her.

She reached for her pulling her close and Mary helped when Alex rolled her atop of her. "What are you—"

"Ride me."

Shaking and half drowned as she was by pleasure, Mary was quick to surface from her stupor. If her beautiful wife asked her to ride her then she was not so foolish as to turn the pleasure of it away. She put shaking hands on Alex's shoulder and with a tentative roll of her hips began a slow and undulating ascent back up the mountain of pleasure she knew awaited. And this time it was even more lovely than the first, because this time it was a journey Alex took with her. Together they moved, bodies fitting as if shorn from the same cloth, and together the wives arrived with cries of love, fulfillment and most importantly—joy.

They lay together panting in the afterglow of their lovemaking, naked and sated, unashamed in their intimacy and for the first time in her life Mary knew that she had been made for such a moment as this, for a woman such as this and that nothing would ever take this new found serenity from her.

At long last Minnie Sophia Pierce had come home and home was the shape of the woman beside her.

THANK YOU!

Thank you for reading Mary and Alex's love story. This story was one that I did not expect to write. It surprised me in the very best of ways and I am so happy to share it with y'all. It has been so wonderful continuing to expand the world of Gold Sky and this is the first of a few planned novellas further expanding the place I have come to love so dearly.

Sign up for our newsletter e-mail list at https://bit.ly/2PCKCZl and *don't be shy about reaching out through social media! I pretty much live for that stuff.*

   Reviews help eager readers find new authors to love and I welcome all reviews, both positive and constructive. Drop me a shout and I'll love y'all to the moon and back!

ABOUT THE AUTHOR

Rebel Carter *loves* love. So much in fact that she decided to write the love stories she desperately wanted to read. A book by Rebel means diverse characters, sexy banter, a real big helping of steamy scenes, and, of course, a whole lotta heart.

Rebel lives in Colorado, makes a mean espresso, and is hell-bent on filling your bookcase with as many romance stories as humanly possible!

ALSO BY REBEL CARTER

Heart and Hand: Interracial Mail Order Bride Romance (Gold Sky Series Book 1)

Hearth and Home: Interracial Mail Order Groom Romance (Gold Sky Series Book 2)

Honor and Desire: Friends to Lovers Romance (Gold Sky Series Book 3)

Three to Love: Interracial Ménage Romance (Gold Sky Book 4)

Love and Gravity: Multicultural STEM Romance

New Girl in Town: Older Woman Younger Man Romance

Auld Lang Syne: Highlands Holiday Novella

Made in the USA
Coppell, TX
04 May 2021

55022111R00090